Lock Down Publications and Ca$h
Presents

I0680251

CRIME PAYS

Lesson One
The Price Of FAME
Fuck All My Enemies

By
Self Made Tay

First Edition 2023

Printed in the United States of America

This is a work of fiction. Names, characters, places, and incidents either
are products of the author's imagination or are used fictitiously. Any
similarity to actual events or locales or persons, living or dead, is
entirely coincidental.

Lock Down Publications
P.O. Box 944
Stockbridge, GA 30281
www.lockdownpublications.com

Like our page on Facebook: Lock Down Publications
www.facebook.com/lockdownpublications.ldp

Stay Connected with Us!

Text **LOCKDOWN** to 22828 to stay up-to-date with new releases, sneak peaks, contests and more…

Like our page on Facebook:
Lock Down Publications

Join Lock Down Publications/The New Era Reading Group

Visit our website:
www.lockdownpublications.com

Follow us on Instagram:
Lock Down Publications

Email Us: We want to hear from you!

Acknowledgements

On all of my acknowledgements I shouted out a list full of people. Not to take anything away from the names that was mentioned because they were well deserved. But this time, I want to unselfishly give a shout out to myself. It was plenty of times, probably just like you, that I wanted to give up. Didn't think I'd make it. Thought I was too weak to continue on. Until I dug deep inside and found true inspiration. The spirit of myself. Ever since I've been tapped in, I've been locked in. So, I want to show appreciation to self for continuously putting up with my bullshit, every time that I had lost focus or fell off track. I will never allow myself to fall victim to a mediocre mind frame again. I promise to always push myself and make all the dreams in my visions come into fruition. I hope that my ambition is strong enough to motivate someone who just needs to know that they can do it. And that "it" is anything and everything you put your mind to. I hope you enjoy the story and I appreciate the support. Hope to catch you on the sequel. With an abundance of gratitude, Thank You. From, Self Made Tay.

Get To Know The Author
Contact Self Made Tay
FB: IMade Tay
IG: Self Made Tay

LESSON 1.1
Work Hard, Play Harder

It was New Year's Eve. The last day, ticking down to the last hour of the 2022 year. "Keem, oh my God! It hurts so good." A woman named Roxy moaned in a painful pleasure. On all fours with her ass up in the air, she took all of Keem's eight-inch length dick in between her bust open pink pussy lips that was so wet it dripped like lemonade.

"Shut up, bitch," Keem ordered as he laid a heavy tap to Roxy's right ass cheek causing it to jiggle like Jello. "You better take this dick like you take them payments. You hear me, bitch?"

"Yes, daddy!" was her only response verbally. Physically though she responded by throwing her light skin red ass back twice as hard. She even threw in a circular rotation every now and then in an attempt to make Keem cum quicker.

Roxy always loved the sexual encounters she had with Keem because the nigga gave her some of the best dick that she'd ever had. He was most definitely in her top three. The one thing that sometimes pissed her off about Keem was that the nigga would take forever to cum. And he hated condoms. So, when he did, he would always leave her pussy full of semen. Other than that, no complaints at all. Besides, better than the dick were the payments.

Keem was a baller. A hustler. A money magnet. The nigga would hands down do anything for a dollar. Sell drugs, rob, steal, and kill. Hell, it was even a time when the nigga held a job down for an eighteen-month run. It was mostly a front for his federal probation papers. Killing two birds with one stone, the job helped him get off papers. And he was able to save up some bread to get on his feet. Truth be told, Roxy had some of the best pussy he'd ever had. Therefore, he never tripped on paying her the thousands of dollars she requested at a time. In his mind, he wasn't paying for the pussy. He fucked bitches for free all the time. Slutted them out and sent them on their way. Letting the sixty minutes of fame go to their heads. Making them feel slightly more important than they actually were.

The difference with Roxy was that she was most likely on all the hitters hit list. She knew her worth for what it was worth. So, she wasn't going that easy. Unless a nigga was willing to come out of pocket before he came out his dick. Keem had no problem at all with skipping the game to get straight to the point. He'd leave all that playing around, zodiac guessing, nursery rhyme riddling shit to the tight pocket, ass broke niggas. All the real players knew it wasn't tricking if you had it. And Keem had it.

"Aww shit. This pussy so damn good, girl!" Keem expressed finally approaching his climax.

"You love this pussy, don't you, daddy?" Roxy teased with a hiss of words.

"Fuck yeah, bitch. You know I love this pussy!" Keem took both of his hands using them to grasp a palm full of Roxy's ass cheeks on both sides. Squeezing them firmly and lifting her ass up towards her lower back. Exposing more of her fat pink pussy. The sight of his dick enter and exit her pussy, in addition to the feeling of ecstasy, caused Keem to almost faint. He leaned in a little closer and wiggled every inch of his dick inside her pussy. "Aww shit. That shit…"

"Yes, daddy! Cum all up inside this pussy, pleasse!" Roxy practically begged, already knowing what time it was.

Keem pulled his dick out slowly one more time and shoved it back in her pussy hole like a shovel in the dirt.

Releasing every seed that waited to escape his nut sack. "Ugghhh." Keem released a moan that you would have thought came from a grizzly bear. Then he collapsed on top of Roxy's backside. "Damn."

"'Bout time," Roxy said, laying on the side of her face, looking back at Keem smiling.

"No bullshit." Keem laid there melting in her warm pussy.

"You need help gettin' out or…?" Roxy asked playfully with a laugh.

"Huh? Oh, naw." Keem laughed a little himself. "Naw, I got it." He planted a gentle kiss to Roxy's cheek and enjoyed the sensation of removing his now medium erected penis from her wetness. Keem sat on the edge of the bed and reached to the floor for his Balmain jeans. Going into his pants pocket, he pulled out what was almost close to forty bands.

In the midst of his counting to five thousand, Roxy went to the bathroom, returning with a hot, damp rag. She used it to clean up the juices that soaked his dick. For a hot second Keem paused his count and let the thought marinate. He loved when Roxy used the rag to clean his dick up.

Exceeding his limit of the count, Keem stopped at six bands and handed them all over to Roxy. "A lil' some extra fo' da holidays. Happy New Year."

"Ooohhh. A Christmas bonus and a New Year's bonus. I'm feeling special-special." Roxy was excited. "Hold off on that happy New Years though, 'cause we ain't make it yet. So don't jinx me. Get back at me in 2023 when it's safe."

Keem stood his five feet nine-inch body frame up. One leg at a time, he slid on his Balmain stitches. "SShidd… I'on kno' what you talkin' 'bout," he said, buckling up his Off-White belt. "I'm to da good out here. It's always safe fo' me, 'cause I'm da main one bringin' da danger." As he spoke, he tucked his Glock .23 with the extended clip underneath his belt. Afterwards he slipped on his Off-White sneakers, then covered his chest with his Balmain shirt.

Roxy sat on the edge of the bed with her thick thighs crossed one on top of the other. The shaved downward triangle that slipped in between her thighs was admiring. Her feet were clean and flawless. Moisturized not dry. Her toenails were freshly pedicured. The paint matched the color on her manicured fingernails. Peach and tan. "Boy, I know who you is." She confirmed. "I'm just sayin'. You know niggas out der itchin' for that last and first kill of da year. So, stay dangerous. As you say."

"Already. That's no question." Keem wasn't worried at all. He'd already been through hell and back twice. Besides, it wasn't a nigga he was worried about. For the most part, niggas stayed in line when it came to Keem. For him, it was one of his biggest fears. But even the opposite sex knew that he wouldn't hesitate to put a few extra holes in a bitch. The Apple ring tone sang from the latest iPhone. Keem got the phone from his pocket. He took a look at the screen. The name of the contact read *Mac*. "Yo." Keem answered.

"I'm hopin' that this would be da one-time that you didn't plan to make a late entrance," Mac said from the phone. His background was so loud. You could hear the music blasting along with the sounds of chatter. Keem knew then that Mac was already at the club. "You need to be here at least twenty minutes before the ball drops in order fo' the mission to go as planned. Where are you?"

"Don't trip, Mac. I'll be der in perfect timing," Keem responded.

"You better, or it'll all be fo' none."

As soon as Keem hung up, someone came banging at Roxy's bedroom door. "Who da fuck is it?" Roxy and Keem both screamed together.

"Ayee, Keem! Come on, maine. We gotta go! What? You in der makin' love to that bitch or somethin'?" On the outside of the door was P. The bitch he was referring to, Roxy of course, was actually his sister.

"Who da fuck you callin' a bitch, pussy? With yo soft ass," Roxy shot back.

"Bitch, shut yo dick-ridin' ass up! You hoe!" P yelled.

"Yeah well, I guess that makes both of us. Now get da fuck away from my door."

"Fuck you bitch!" P shouted as his voice faded off into the distance. You could tell that he was walking down the hallway.

"Y'all ass crazy." Keem always found the siblings' interactions entertaining.

"I can't stand his ass," Roxy reminded Keem for the hundredth time.

The feeling was mutual with P. He hated his sister with a passion. He respected her ambition to get to the bag but hated the route she took in addition to the disrespect that he thought it brought on herself. It also brings back bad memories from their childhood. Their mother used to do the exact same thing. Only ten times worst. For ten times less. Deep down though, P knew that he couldn't blame Roxy for taking on the only family business that they had. He just wished that she would exit that lane before she crashed. He wanted better for his younger sister. It pissed him off that she acted as if she could give two fucks.

A couple minutes later, Keem and P were hopping into Keem's 2023 Range Rover. Keem never liked to talk during a trip. He always preferred to replace the silence with the music. Blasting his six twelve speakers. He raised the volume to Future, Gunna, and Young Thug's summer smash *Pushing P*.

Speaking of P's. P's real name was Rick. He was from a neighborhood called the Heights out of Petersburg, Virginia, which, if you haven't figured out by now, is what lead his alias to being simply P. Another way was the fact that he pushed a great good number of pounds of nothing but the best pressure through the city of Petersburg. One day Keem ran into P in pursuit of the gas and stumbled upon a gold mine. Or should I say green? Anyway, Keem helped P expand his business into the bigger city of Richmond. In return, all Keem wanted was to hook up with P's sister. The very first time he laid eyes on her, safe to say, P wasn't only pushing pounds of pressure but he also lent a hand in helping his sister push her pussy. Hypocrite. Guess a nigga will throw away all his morals for the price of fame.

Keem overseeded the speed limit by almost twenty miles per hour, shorting the trip from Petersburg to Richmond down to about twenty minutes. At 11:30, the night had just begun.

LESSON 1.2
Trust Nobody

Accompanied by P, Keem pulled up to Club Jungle. He hopped out and threw his keys to the valet. "You scratch my shit, yo ass gone die."

"Shut up, nigga. I know how to drive, fool. How you think I got da job, stupid?" The young 20 years of age valet questioned.

"'Cause I put yo ass on," Keem reminded him.

"Yeah, how could I eva forget with you remindin' me every chance you get?"

Keem didn't even bother to stop nor answer the question asked.

"Ayee Keem!" The young valet shouted. "Let me take this bitch for a spin right quick, big brah?"

"Do you," was Keem's reply. "Matta fact, gas it up. Hold it down fo' da next twenty-four hours. I'll hit you when it's time to cough it back up. And tell ma I said I love her when you get home."

"Shid... I'on think I'm goin' home fo' da next twenty-four hours wit dis mafucka," the young'in said to himself excitingly.

The valet was Keem's younger brother by seven years. Keem's objective was to keep his little brother, Shy, of the streets. That was his reason for putting in a word, providing him with the valet job at Club Jungle, even though the job paid more than fairly for a twenty-year-old young man,

11

especially coming from poverty. What Keem failed to realize was that the more he blew up, the more Shy grew in admiration to become exactly like his older brother.

Keem and P walked up to the front of the long line.

"Ayee, Keem! This Slow, my nigga. Let me go in with you?"

"Aye, Keem, can you pay my way, please?" A woman in the line yelled.

Walking around the metal detectors, Keem's celebrity only intensified. They celebrated Keem's entrance as if he was the new year itself. Keem took a look at his big face bust down bezel. 11:38PM. "Like I said, perfect timing with a few minutes to spare."

"Day one, what's up?" Keem's sandbox friend approached him head on.

"Ace! What's good, fool?" Keem replied embracing his friend. "Everything A-one, my nigga?"

"Hell yeah. Since day one, fool." Ace pulled Keem in closer so he could hear his next few words clearly without any misunderstanding. "Since we was kids, you always said that you would get us here. And you did. I love you for life, my nigga."

"Already, nigga. Love for life." Keem stamped the love as they unleashed their embrace. "Aye, look, Ace, I'm 'bout to buy da bar out for da rest of da night. So, drink up. But I need you to meet me at da photo booth in ten minutes. We 'bout to go da fuck in!"

"Ight. Bet, fool. Say no more."

So, Keem said no more. Instead, he did as he said he would and headed over to the bar to buy it out. He grabbed him a bottle of his favorite, D'ussé, and sent sparkling bottles of Ace of Spades around to random people. Once the DJ made the announcement that the bar was on the house for the rest of the night, most of the crowd rushed toward it.

Keem looked up to the second floor of the club and could see the owner staring down at him. Mac watched his prodigy with intensified focus. Mac had a liking for Keem that he didn't even have for his own son. It was mainly his loyalty that attracted Mac to Keem. And he wasn't talking about his loyalty to certain people. But the loyalty that Keem gave to himself and to the game he played in. Mac nodded towards Keem. Keem threw a salute back in response before heading up the stairs.

"Sup, Big Dawg?" Keem barked over the loud music, entering the VIP section of the club. He stood beside Mac and leaned over the balcony getting a full overview vision of the club. Keem felt big in his position at the moment but was smart and humble enough to know that he still had a long way to go. While everyone else in the club was there to celebrate by partying and turning up, he was there for only one reason. And that reason was to level up. Tonight, he would show Mac just how bad he wanted the game in the palm of his hands.

"I see you made it in a timely fashion," Mac said actually happy about Keem's appearance.

"Come on now, Mac." Keem's response seemed to have been touched with a boast of bragging. "Name one time I've eva let you down."

"You got that one. That's why I know that I can count on you. But it's still my job to keep you rug rats on yo toes."

"Yeah, I feel that. But I'ma keep it G with you. Not only am I doing this for you, or da game, ova all I'm doin' this shit for me." Keem pounded his right fist on his chest.

"I know. That's another reason why I fucks with you da G way. You always put yo' self first. I've never seen a nigga as selfish as me, other den you."

Keem laughed.

In the next ten minutes, Keem had only a half full bottle of D'ussé left. And that was a bottle that he always refused to share. Heading back down the stairs from the second floor of the club, Keem made his way to the DJ booth. Whispering in the DJ's ear he made a special request. As requested, the

DJ switched songs and played *Before I Go* by Kodak Black featuring Rod Wave. After shouting Keem out over the microphone, the DJ called out for P and Ace to meet up at the back of the club where the photo booth was held. It was time for the photo shoot. Everything was falling into place perfectly. A few other members of the gang, along with a handful of baddies, all crowded in front of the backdrop of the photo booth. In about five minutes of timing, the photographer snapped well over a dozen pictures.

"Ayee, ight everybody, let me get a couple joints with just me and my day one," Keem demanded.

No one protested. Keem and Ace took a few pictures holding bottles of Ace and bands so large that they could barely be held within their hands.

"Ight now everybody," the DJ screamed over the mic. "Da two-minute warnin' is approachin' and da countdown to a new year is about to begin. I hope everyone is ready to leave all da bullshit in 2022 and level up with me in this 23! I'll get back with you in about one hundred seconds."

"Aye, Ace." Keem wrapped his arm around Ace's neck, safely cuffing him underneath his wing. "Rock with me right quick. We gotta handle some business."

Ace didn't refuse. He never did when it came to Keem. With all the attention on the dance floor or the bar, the crowded club awaited the ball to drop. Going unnoticed, Keem and Ace slipped out the back door of the club, landing them in a dark alleyway.

Stepping out into the brisk midnight winter air, Ace shivered. He paused for a quick second or two when he noticed an all-black bucket of a vehicle parked in the alley. "Who da fuck would be dumb enough to park back here?" Ace asked the obvious.

"Exactly," Keem agreed. "Probably some dick head who was up to no good."

CRIME PAYS | SELF MADE TAY

Even when standing in the alley Keem and Ace could hear the crowd of people shouting out the numbers to the count down. *"Ten, nine, eight, seven…"*

"Come on, nigga!" Ace urged Keem. "What da fuck is we back here for, my nigga? Shit, we 'bout to miss da ball droppin'."

"Six, five, four…"

"Naw, you ain't missing nothin', my nigga." Keem assured. "Trust me." By the end of his sentence, Keem was whipping out his Glock from underneath his Off-White designer belt.

As soon as Ace noticed what was taking place, he went to reach for his own gun out of pure instinct and habit. That's when he remembered he was naked. "Yo, Keem, what da fuck goin' on, my dude?"

"Three, two, one…" Bow! *"Happy New Year!"* The whole city of Richmond erupted in a union of celebration. However, before the ball could even drop in New York, Ace's body had already dropped to the ground, making 2022 his last and final living year.

Keem stared down at the corpse of Ace. "I told you since day one, my nigga. It's rules to this shit. And it's two different sides of da same rules. Those that make 'em and those that break 'em. den you got da ones that stay in da middle and actually obey 'em. You can cheat life. But you can't cheat death. Hope you learnt yo' lesson, my friend. 'Til we meet again, fool. Rest up." Keem stepped over his best friend's body and headed to the bucket which was his getaway car. The ringtone to Ace's phone was non-stop. Calls were coming in back-to-back. Keem hopped in the car and pulled off slowly without a care in the world. After all, he felt as if the world was his.

LESSON 1.3
Hold Your Own

Rewinding about ten minutes before the ball dropped, about ten miles north of Shockoe Bottom, where club Jungle was located, on the corner of Fairfield Avenue and Mechanicsville Turnpike sat a convenience store that stayed open twenty-four hours seven days a week. On the side of that store awaited four young thugs. BM, the leader of the bunch, was accompanied by E who was his right-hand man. Then there was Ike and Ron. The two were cousins.

"Y'all niggas better be ready for this shit," BM gassed, speaking just above a whisper under his all-black ski mask that matched the all-black everything else that he had on. "I'm tellin' y'all now, don't trick this shit up 'cause I ain't pickin' up niggas' slack. We gone go in this bitch, get all da money and anything else that's highly valuable. We bringin' in this new year with some bands. Fuck All that broke shit."

"Shid… let's go den, nigga." Ike spoke up from underneath his black bandana that was tied around his face. "As soon as you shut da fuck up we'll be able to handle our business."

"Say no more den, killa," BM said sarcastically, knowing that he and E were the only two present that ever actually murdered a man in cold blood.

Ike though, was a robbery fanatic. That's all he knew. So that's all he did. Only thing was that all of his licks were very mediocre. This would be the biggest robbery he'd ever pulled. To say the least, he was both hungry and thirsty. Ron was only there because when BM and E had pulled up on Ike inviting him on the lick as a third wheel, Ike put up a bluff that he wouldn't go unless he was able to bring his cousin Ron as a tag along. They went for the bluff and here they were.

BM led the way into the store, rushing in with his gun held high, headed straight toward the cashier. "I swear to God, bitch! Yo ass better not move or it's a wrap for yo ass," BM threatened. "Now open that bitch and give me everything up in that mafucka fo' I open yo mafuckin' brains up!"

"Ight, alright my friend." The cashier complied. "Please don't hurt me. I have family." The cashier was an Arab whose face was covered in long black, silky hair that had a few strokes of grayness. His hands were raised up in the air. Due to fear he hesitated to make a move to the cash register, thinking that any wrong move could have him gunned down.

Ron stood watch at the door as planned. E stuck by BM's side as he always did throughout any situation. And Ike was growing impatient.

Bow! A single shot flew past the head of the Arab causing him to duck out of survival instinct. "Nigga, hurry da fuck up," Ike demanded, "'for we kill yo ass like he said! I promise you da next one I won't miss."

"What da fuck you doin', nigga?" BM questioned Ike. "You makin' shit hot." But that wasn't the only thing that had BM pissed off. It was in addition to the fact that Ike had the nerve to try and take over his operation.

"What?" Ike asked in self-defense. "Da nigga wasn't movin'. We don't have time to sit right here and play with this nigga. We need to get it and go."

"Aye, brah." BM nudged E, who was still by his side, with his elbow. "Take this nigga." E knew that he meant Ike. "And y'all niggas fill up da bags with da goods. I got this up here."

Without saying a word, E did what he was told. Snatching up Ike, together they bagged any and everything that had the most value. Liquors, foods, clothing, tobacco products, lottery tickets, cell phones, whatever. If the shit could be sold and would fit in the bag, it was theirs.

"Ight, look here, old man. Steady and slowly. Get yo ass up." BM demanded the man. "I'm tryin' to be nice and it's not workin' out well for me. Now open da fuckin' cash register and put da money on da counter 'for I smoke yo ass and do da shit my-damn-self."

"Okay, Okay. I'm moving." The store owner did what he was told. In mostly all ones, fives, tens, along with a few twenties he laid almost three hundred dollars' worth of cash on the countertop.

"What you think I'm stupid or somethin', mafucka?" BM leaned over the counter and struck the man over the head with the gun. "Where da real money at? What's up under that ma fucka?"

The man was frightened to death. Going through his mind though was how much longer it would be.

"Ayee, brah, I think we need to hurry up," Ron said, still standing at the door looking out.

"I ain't leavin' this bitch without some real money. Or a mafuckin' body." BM let it be known.

"Yeah but—"

"Nigga, shut da fuck up!" BM shouted at Ron. "And you," he said immediately turning his attention back to the cashier. "Hurry da fuck up!" BM was right. He knew who he was from the beginning. That was the whole reason he picked this store. For nineteen years since he was old enough to walk he was a shopper at this store. He knew exactly where the big bills were.

Lifting up the tray to the cash register the man laid up to three thousand dollars' worth of cash on the counter in all fifties and hundreds. "Okay. You have money now. Can you please go? Just leave."

"Naw, fuck that." BM was feeling lucky. "Where da mafuckin' safe at? I know you holdin' more than dis."

Before the man could even lie about not having a safe, a loud thud came from a door being burst wide open from the back of a small deli area. Right after the thud was the sound of a cocking shotgun followed by the blast of the pellets being released. The smell of gun powder filled the air quickly. The close-range shot damn near left a hole in Ike's stomach. If he wasn't hungry before, he definitely would be left with an empty stomach now. Before his knees could even touch the ground, another cock and another blast. This time the shot took off Ike's face. It's no need to say it, but it was over for him.

From the front of the store, Ron heard the commotion and witnessed the blast light up his cousin like the Fourth of July. Allowing his emotions to move him, he rushed to the back of the store to Ike as if he could save him.

The slamming of the opening door caught BM off guard. On instinct he took a quick look back, nervous that it may have been him who was the target. Either way it went, it was a great mistake. The Arab behind the counter reached down for his concealed weapon and raised it up, exposing his .357 long nose revolver. *Vow! Vow!* The gun barked, damn near knocking BM off his feet without a bullet even touching him. Just the thought of being touched by one had BM's life flashing before his eyes.

Throwing blind shots behind his back, E ran away from the shotgun blaster leaving Ike to carry his own weight. On his way to the front of the store, he was bumped by Ron who was heading exactly to the spot he was avoiding. Losing his balance, E stumbled to the floor while Ron kept it moving in a rush. Ending up on the floor somehow worked out well for E though. At least down there he was able to duck the shots that came from the front of the store.

Snapping out of panic mode BM bounced back by throwing shots back at the cashier. The three shots were to no avail. The aim of BM was so off that the target neither attempted to duck nor dodge. Instead, he threw back three more shots of his own. Luckily for BM the last shot flew straight past his chin, coming close to knocking his chin off his face. Unfortunately, though, that same bullet smashed him in the left shoulder causing him to crash into the potato chip stand.

By the time Ron had made it to his cousin Ike, he realized just how stupid the idea of trying to save an already dead man was. For one, not only was he already dead of course, but once he looked up to Ike's murderer, he realized that he was the next to go. The shotgun blast blew Ron a few steps back in the direction he had just come from. They were close cousins to a tight knit family. I'm pretty sure this New Years would be a hard one for their bloodline.

Hearing the shotgun roar once more, E decided to recover quickly and get back to his feet. He sent shots flying to the front of the store. The man behind the cash register was caught off guard. Plus, the aim was decent. Putting the Arab in defense mode, that gave E just enough time to head towards the door. On his way out, he had to go past his injured friend. He figured, what the hell; gripping BM by his shirt while still in motion. "Come on, nigga! Let's fuckin' go!" E yelled. He ain't have to say it twice.

BM's legs moved expeditiously. E shot towards the man that was ducked behind the counter, daring him to pop back up again. In the other direction, BM let off plenty of aimless wildfire shots from his thirty-round clip. It was totally due to defense rather than fear caused by the biggest fright he'd ever felt in his life. The man carrying the shotgun took aim with the only intent to kill. Thankful for the two comrades, BM's shots advised him to thank twice. With just that one thought of hesitation, BM and E were able to make it out of the store alive; pants sagging, hall-assing for their lives.

BM and E had silently said fuck their original plan of taking the long and smarter route back to the hood. They cut across the wide intersection of Mechanicsville Turnpike and Fairfield Way, heading straight to their Mosby Court projects residents. Zooming through Accommodation Street like track stars they ran into a cul-de-sac. Going around to the rear end of the building, they entered the back door to a vacant project apartment they called their trap.

Being the fastest on his feet, and even though he wouldn't admit it, the scariest. With his adrenaline rushing like a crack head on ecstasy, BM was the first one through the door. "Make sure you lock that joint," he reminded E.

They took a seat at the table that was placed in an almost empty kitchen. For a moment it was complete silence between the two. All that was heard was the combination of ambulance and police sirens.

"That bitch ass nigga shot me," BM said. The pain was evident through his voice. Gripping his shoulder tight to stop the blood he winced. "Aww, shit! I'ma kill that bitch, watch."

"Shid… at least we made it out that ma'fucka still breathin'."

"Nigga, that's easy for you to say 'cause yo ass ain't da one with a hole in yo shoulder."

E gave BM a puzzled look. "Brah, Ike got his fuckin' face blown off. It's gone. A closed casket for that nigga."

"Good," BM said surprising the fuck out of E. "That nigga fuckin' deserved to die." E grew even more confused but said nothing. "It's that nigga fault that all this shit happened anyway. If his dumb ass wouldn't have never let of da first shot, da shit would've stayed a robbery instead of turning into a double homicide. And it's yo fault that da nigga was even der in da first place."

"What? My fault?"

"Yeah, nigga! What? You forgot it was yo dumb ass idea to ask da nigga to go on da lick with us?"

"Naw, I ain't forget. But if da idea was so fuckin' dumb, please explain to me why yo dumb ass agreed to it?"

21

"'Cause, nigga, I wanted to use them niggas as crash dummies." BM paused for a quick half of a second after he admitted. "As a matta fact. I'm glad them niggas was der, 'cause if dey wasn't, den maybe it would have been me that was left faceless. So yeah, I guess I am smart after all."

"Whateva, nigga. While you talkin' all that shit with yo smart ass, you might need to go to da hospital 'for yo ass bleed out and die right der in that chair. Sittin' der talkin shit."

"You really think I'm 'bout to go to da hospital? You must be tryin' to get me out da way or some."

"Aye, tighten up, brah. Don't come at me like I'm some snake ass nigga or some. All I'm tryin' to do is make sure my nigga is good."

"You know damn well them people gone link me to that robbery-slash-shootin' somehow. Fuckin' Arabs probably ran down da whole fuckin' story by now. You better bet dey lookin' for a nigga my height, my size, and color to show up to da hospital lookin' to get treated for a bullet wound to da left shoulder."

"We don't gotta go to MCV. If we leave now, we can go somewhere outside da city. Hanover or Petersburg somewhere. It's options."

"We don't even have a car, dick head."

"Call a Uber or Lyft."

For a few long seconds BM looked at E with a stupid facial expression that said *"really"* written all over it. Seemed as if time moved extra slowly before BM spoke again. "You really are a dumb ass, huh? I ain't callin' no fuckin' Uber, stupid. I might as well dial 9-1-1 myself for all that."

"Well, let's—"

"Look," BM shouted, cutting E off. "No more of yo stupid ass ideas, please. On gang, brah, you makin' me wish I was dead already. Whateva type of treatment I'ma get, we gone have to do ourselves."

"What? Nigga, I ain't no doctor."

"Obviously not. Just help me get some of des clothes off so we can at least take a look at da wound." Together and slowly E assisted BM with taking his left arm out of the sleeve of the hoody. "Aww... fuck!" The pain made BM suck his teeth. Something he hated to do. Off came the sleeve of the sweater. The thermal shirt came next.

"You might as well take all this shit off," E suggested, already preparing to pull all the tops over his head.

"Naw. Naw. Naw. Hell naw!" BM denied. "I might have to go back outside or somethin'."

"Go back outside for what?" E questioned. "We good in here, nigga. And you know da blade on fire right now."

"Shid, you never know, fool. What if them people hit da spot?"

"Yeah, I guess you right." E just let the thought go over his head without any further protest. The last level of clothing that still covered the wound was the worst part. The sleeve to the all-black tee shirt stuck to the white meat of the wound. "Ight, hold on, brah. This shit might hurt like a mafucka. But I'ma have to pull da sleeve ova yo shoulda in order to see da joint."

"Ight. Maine, whateva. Just do whateva da fuck you gotta do."

E begun to roll up the sleeve as slowly as possible trying not to cause his friend any more pain than he was already in.

"Nigga, hurry da fuck up!" BM yelled out the blue causing E to jump a little. E said nothing in return. What he did was exactly what he was told. When the shirt separated from the wound it put BM in a state of excruciating pain. "Aww! Bitch!

"Shut yo tough ass up, pussy. You da one that told me to hurry up."

"Nigga, I said, 'hurry da fuck up!'"

"Ight, brah, chill on me right quick. Let me see how bad it looks."

BM tried his best to settle down in attempt to endure the pain. As he did, E was able to take a closer look.

"Nigga." E sucked his teeth. "That shit went straight through yo' shoulda."

"I knew my back felt wet." BM confirmed. "I thought I was hit twice."

"Naw, fool, you good." E assured him. "You in here doin' all that bitchin' fo' nothin'."

"Da fuck up, nigga. You was doin' mo' cryin' den me. Talkin' 'bout dyin' and shit. Plus, this shit still hurts... a little. And I'm still gone need somethin' to keep it from gettin' infected, and somethin' to help it heal faster."

They pondered for a few seconds before E came up with his first bright idea in the last few minutes. "I gotta idea."

"Aww great." BM sounded fatigued from the thought of having to hear another one of E's ideas. "Not another one."

"Naw, you gone love this one. It's yo' favorite. Both of 'em." BM was clueless. He sat and waited to find out exactly what E was getting at. He watched as E walked over to one of the kitchen's cabinets and removed something from it. Next, he headed to the refrigerator and came out with a bottle of Lunazul Tequila. He placed the bottle on the table and laid down a quarter ounce of cocaine beside it.

"What da fuck you think you 'bout to do with that shit?"

"Maine, get yo' ass up and come to da sink right quick. You need to get some alcohol on that shit."

"Yeah, but not that kind of alcohol. That shit ain't gone work."

"Shid... yeah it is. I see da shit happen in movies all da time."

"Well, stupid, this ain't no mafuckin' movie. Is it?"

"You know what? You right. You must gone be da one to walk yo' ass to da store and get you a bottle of alcohol?"

BM paused in thought. "Fuck it." He gave in. "Hold on right quick though." He grabbed the sandwich bag containing the cocaine, went into the small of his pocket, and pulled out a card.

"That's what da fuck I'm talkin' 'bout, my nigga," E remarked while growing excited. "Shake that shit da fuck off!"

BM fed both his nostrils with the snow-white powdery substance and abused it. "Ight, let's go. I'm ready." He stood up and made his way over to the kitchen sink.

E assisted him by guiding his shoulders over the sink. "Ight now, brah. I ain't gone lie, this shit might sting just a lil'. It's gone make it better in da long run though."

"Do what you gotta do, fool." E took the bottle in his grasp and dumped gulps of Tequila directly into BM's open wound. His eyes immediately closed tight from the pain and a couple tears dripped from the corners. He hissed like a snake trying to stop the saliva from running out of his mouth. "Aaawww." The expression of pain that came from his mouth was said in a low tone. His heartbeat doubled. Body became heated from the pain. He was trying his best to contain the anger. Without warning, E dumped more liquor over his shoulder making sure to cover both the back and front side of the wound. Even though he was unprepared and caught off guard, BM took the healing liquid a little better the second time.

"That should be enough I guess." E assumed.

"Fuck yeah, that's enough!" BM spat and went back to his seat at the kitchen table. E used a dry rag to dry up the dripping alcohol around the wound. "You can let da rest of that shit air dry brah, for real." BM suggested. "That shit startin' to feel good for real, nigga; on my mama." He sunk down some, slopping in the chair as his eyes started flickering its lids.

"Here, nigga," E placed a small, round bluish green tablet in front of BM. "Dis shit gone really help take da pain away." It was a 30-miligram Percocet.

BM's eyes widened at the sight of the pill. Already having an addiction to the drug, he knew exactly what it would do to him. He threw the pill back and swallowed it down with a swig of liquor. After that, E did the same.

For some time, it was all silence. The thought of a happy new year was the farthest thing from either of the young goons' mind. As a matter of fact, they had forgotten all about a new year altogether. They'd been tight all their lives. Like the middle and index fingers wrapped around each other. And although murder was their best street talent, they were still thick as thieves.

E stood up from his chair and walked over to his friend.

"What da hell you doin', nigga?" BM asked. Every other twenty to thirty seconds he had nodded out. Yet, every second of the minutes that passed, he kept his guard up.

"Dis da final stage of my treatment idea," E concluded. "Not sure if it'll do any good. But I know it won't hurt none." He already had the bag of cocaine in his hand. "I'ma just sprinkle a lil' bit of this on yo' shit and see what it do."

BM had thoughts but didn't say a word. E took the card, dipped it in the bag, and proceeded with his plan. The drug caused no harm. It only numbed it even more than it already felt.

"Shid… my nigga. Maybe you should have been a doctor." BM thought out loud.

"How da hell I'ma be a doctor with felonies on my record since I was fourteen years old?"

"Ion know. I'm just sayin'. Maybe you should've never jumped off da porch with a nigga like me."

"With a nigga like you?" E almost felt offended. "Wat da fuck thats supposed to mean? Nigga, I am a nigga like you."

"Naw, fool. You ain't nothin' like me."

"Oh yeah? Well, please, tell me da difference." BM had no reply. "Exactly, like da fuck I thought."

But it wasn't because he didn't have the answer. It was just that he was too ashamed to admit it and didn't think it would be smart to expose his own hand.

"Anyway, nigga, what's up with that bread? What we came up on?" E was ready to get to the business.

"I'on know. I ain't count yet."

"Ight, nigga. Well, get da money out and let's get to countin'."

BM's silence followed by E's suggestion alarmed him that something wasn't right. If nobody knew when BM was up to something, E knew. And BM was definitely up to something. His subconscious mind was telling him to go for his gun. But he battled with the thought of pulling out a weapon on his one and only friend for no justified reason. Or so he thought.

BM reached under the table with expedience and withdrew his pistol from his pants. Never slowing down his speed, he raised the gun above the table and aimed it at E's chest. *BOCCA! BOCCA!* "See, E," BM stated, rising to his feet. "Da difference is, my nigga, you too loyal to a lifestyle where loyalty doesn't exist." By this time, E had fell backwards in the chair, causing his body to fall to the floor. "Yo heart too big, my nigga." BM walked closer to E with the gun still aimed at him. "It's too much love in . That's why you don't belong. Ain't no love out here, my nigga! God fucked you ova by placin' you in an environment where niggas like me eat off niggas like you."

"Come on, my nigga." E pleaded barely above a whisper. A tear from the pain escaped his eye though it wasn't the pain from the bullets. The pain came from the betrayal of his friend. "After all we been through? Dis wat it is?"

"Dis exactly what it is." *BOCCA! BOCCA! BOCCA!* BM placed three more random shots into E's body. Afterwards, he went into his pockets and took everything he had on him except the gun and a few dimes of crack cocaine. "Fucked up when a drug deal goes wrong." BM let out a sinister chuckle. "Damn, my nigga got robbed by a junkie." BM quickly gathered his thoughts and exited the vacant apartment leaving E to die on his own.

LESSON 1.4
Two Sides of The Same Coin

"What's da take on da night?" A detective by the name of Calvez asked his partner Detective Winchester.

"Well, a couple of officers reported a single shot at Club Jungle," Detective Winchester replied. "False call though. No body was found. No one was injured. That was right before New Year's within a matter of seconds. You know. The regular at midnight. A bunch of shots went off throughout the city." Together the detectives lifted the caution tape and passed through the crime scene.

"Okay," Calvin said. "Nothing unusual. So, what do we have here?" He asked about the double homicide at the store on the East End of the city of Richmond.

"Store owner stated it was a robbery gone bad." They continued walking, approaching the door of the store. "Says it was four total. Also claims that he caught one of them in his shoulder." Detective Winchester walked his partner, who was late to the crime scene, over to one of their main pieces of evidence. "From the footage of the surveillance tapes we pulled from the store." Winchester pointed to a bag of Snack Rap potato chips that had fallen on the floor. "I wanted you to see this before I allowed forensics to bag it and run a sample at the lab. It's the blood of the suspect that caught the bullet to the shoulder." Without saying a word, only using the snap of a finger, Winchester called over a woman from

CRIME PAYS | SELF MADE TAY

the forensics team to come over and gather the evidence. "You can take it now." He ordered the woman.

She snapped a few more pictures from different angles before placing the bag of chips into an evidence bag.

"Back here," Detective Winchester continued as he proceeded to walk further into the store. "We have two suspects turned victims. One is completely unrecognizable by face." He paused as he watched his partner squat with the intention to remove the white sheet from the corpse. "Kid got his face blown off," he announced as soon as his partner pulled back the sheet.

"Umm," Detective Calvez said with a cold shiver while shaking his head.

"We've already started the process of identification." Winchester concluded. "Over here is what we have as the second victim. Unlike that one over there, this one was weaponless. Seems as if he was used as the lookout. The kid's name is Rondell Walker. Eighteen years of age. Actually, turned-out to be a decent kid. No criminal background records. High school graduate who was now working at the McDonald's just down the street. We're reaching out to the kids' family now to break the bad news. Also, to find out more about the kid and figure out exactly why he was running with these other three stooges. Maybe the family could point us in the direction of his friends. But give or take, you know how that goes."

"You've done well, partner." Calvez admitted.

"Learned from the best," Winchester complimented softly, praising his partner of now six years. "You mind letting me in on why you were so late to the show?" He now inquired.

"Just trying to tie Macsby into at least one of the bodies that fell throughout the city for the year 2022. I was out looking for one of his crew members to stumble upon a broken law tonight partying while being overly intoxicated."

"You know like I do that Mac's Mob moves like a turtle. Every single step is calculated."

"Yeah, well, all it takes is that one step. They missed just that one step and that's the shell off the turtle's back." Detective Calvez hated Mac with a passion. Like a Washington Commander hated a Dallas Cowboy fan.

The hatred started well over twenty years ago when the two attended Armstrong High School. Mac was the bully and Calvez was one of many victims. For decades, Calvez planned and plotted a way to revenge his arch rival. Mac being the head boss of a criminal master organization and Calvez being head detective of the East Ends robbery and homicide just so happened to play out perfectly. The only thing was that Mac's motive was mainly drugs. A field that Calvez had no hands, nor say in. But, of course, eventually murder or robbery came with drugs. So Calvez sat, prayed, and waited for that day when Mac's folder officially came across his desk. Until then, he was more than determined to find another way in.

"Okay, let's get these bodies out of here and see if we can get the store owner and every worker present in the store down to the precinct for a more formal questioning." Calvez ordered his younger and a few shades lighter partner against crime. "I'm going to take a closer look around. Get more into the detail of things. You know, get into my criminal mindset. Think like them. Run a couple scenarios down."

"Yes, sir, partner. I'm on it."

"Hey, and youngster." Calvez called out to Winchester before he was even able to start barking orders to the crime scene team.

"Sir," Winchester replied.

"Make sure we get an extra copy of that footage, please."

"Already done, partner."

"You're the best."

The remark from his elder detective left Winchester walking away with a confident smile spread across his face.

Calvez got straight to the business. "Okay, so I'm coming in looking to rob the place," he said to himself in a low tone of voice. "I'm the master mind. But it's four of me. At least one of me is weaponless. There's a gun on the faceless me. Shots over here. Shots spread over there. Yeah, definitely that one. That partion of me should be at the door." He assumed. Mapping the place out as if it were his very own plan to rob the place.

This was Calvez's favorite part of the job. Well, aside from actually cracking the case, of course. But he'd grown up around criminals. For some fortunate reason though, he just never fell in or got along with them. It just never felt right. So, it aroused him in some type of psychotic way whenever he had the chance to play out the criminal in a real-life scene without having to deal with the consequences of the punishments that came with the crime.

Just as he was tricking his mind to think of himself as a suspect in action, he got a call on his cell phone. He reached for it urgently hoping that it was the call that he had expected it to be. "Lieutenant Detective Calvez speaking." He answered. "What do you mean you don't have authorization?" He eagerly questioned the person on the other end of the phone. "I don't give a shit what they say you can or cannot do. I need you to get it done. You gave me your word and I gave you the payment as promised. Now you find a way to make this shit happen or I swear on my own badge that I'll dig so much dirt up on your ass that you would want to bury your damn self in it." Calvez was highly disappointed at whatever whoever on the other side of the phone was telling him. "You better, or…"

"Come in, all units. Shots fired. Mosby Court on Accommodation Street. I repeat, shots fired. Nearby units please respond immediately."

Calvez's threat over the phone was cut short when the dispatcher came over the radio.

"Calvez in pursuit!" The detective tapped into the walkie-talkie after snatching it off his hip. "I repeat, Detective Calvez enroute to location!" He ended the call with the push of the red button on the phone, placed it in his pocket, and hauled ass out of the store. "Winchester! Let's make a move!" He yelled out in no particular direction in hopes that his partner would hear his words. "It's a couple blocks away. May be a connection in the links."

Choosing to leave his car behind in the short distance, Winchester was right there opening the passenger side door to his partner's vehicle. "I'm already with you, partner," he assured, hopping into the car. They drove off into the night in a hurried rush on their way to their second shooting of the fresh new year.

LESSON 1.5

Collect What's Yours

A good eight to nine hours away from the midnight of mayhem, the sun shined above the city of Richmond. Surprisingly, it was a fairly heated day in the start of the winter season. At sixty-six degrees the wind blew as if it was the beginning of spring. "Ayee, yo, Pike! What up?"

A nigga in his mid-twenties the hood referred to as Pike heard a voice call out to him from amongst the shadows. "Who the fuck is that?" Pike questioned as he traveled through a spaced-out alley in the bottom of Mosby Court Projects. Hearing the voice without seeing its source caused Pike to move extra cautiously, placing his hand on the handle of the pistol that rested on his hip.

"It's BM, fool." The person gave a name to its voice. "Right here, nigga," BM confirmed when he noticed Pike struggling to seek him out. "Beside the trash can, brah."

Pike looked down on a porch at the back door where BM sat beside a trash can. From his point of view, all Pike could see was the burgundy number eleven Jordan's, a half set of legs, and now the head of BM peeking around the corner. "Oh," Pike said more relieved than anything to confirm that it wasn't a set up like he ignorantly thought when he heard the voice call his name out. "Nigga, yo ass can't be playin' them type of games."

BM laughed the comment off nonchalantly. "My nigga, you know if I wanted to take it der , yo ass would been soaked up already."

"Yeah. Just like yo ass knew you would have been, too, 'cause to hesitate would have been a suicide move," Pike responded before asking, "Fuck you doin' anyway, nigga?"

"Come here, fool!" BM waved him over. "Sit yo ass down." He offered a seat. Pike accepted without protest. "Here." BM handed him a wad of cash. "That's two bands. I'm tryna get a ounce of the powder and at least twenty grams of the dog food. That good shit, nigga. Not that trash."

"Okay, lil' nigga," Pike said excitedly. "I see you done came up ova night, huh? Nigga ain't playin' no games this year, is it? I got you. I'ma get you straight. But why the fuck you ain't just hit my line, fool?"

"Shid... gotta get a new phone. I'ma do that today though. Soon as I do, I'ma shoot you a text so you can lock my number in."

"Already, fool." Pike said. "Ayee, but look, though. I ask everybody this same shit. I like to give niggas dey options. You feel me?"

"Ight. What we talkin' 'bout though?"

"You want that straight dope or that fentanyl?"

"Shid... nigga, you know damn well that fentanyl move like water goin' downhill." BM answered.

"Already. Just had to make sure. Some of des niggas be scared of that naly." Pike admitted.

"Shid, I ain't scared of no money. If dey gone come and buy it, I'ma sell it."

"That's definitely what the streets want. And dey comin' back-to-back for that shit. I'ma get this shit togeder for you. But before I do, what the hell happened to yo right hand man last night? Niggas sayin' he got plugged last night on Combo. Say he might not make it through and some more shit?"

35

BM heard the question loud and clear but ignored it for the moment due to the statement that followed. What the fuck did he mean '*might not make it through?*' BM wasn't even aware until just then that he had even left E with the option to live. His blood pressure increased a little. Just right beneath his boiling point. Not only did he have to take a mark away from his body count but he'd now have to watch over his shoulders even more now. He knew, just like everyone else did, that E was not to be played with. It was true that he had a big heart and that he was a good nigga, but if ever crossed that same love turned evil. And the same heart he loved from, he'd use to kill.

"BM! You heard me nigga?" Pike slightly raised his voice, snapping BM out of his thoughts.

"Huh?" BM jumped a little. "Yeah, I heard you, brah. Shit just had me stuck 'cause I ain't even know my nigga was hit." BM Immediately began to put his lie together. "That shit do explain why I ain't heard from the nigga all day."

"That's what I'm sayin'. That nigga would usually be out here with you. I'm surprised you ain't heard though. The whole projects talkin' 'bout the shit."

"Naw, brah. I've been right here for real. Dey ain't know who hit 'em though?" It was smart for BM to keep his ears close to the streets. He needed to be the first to know if he was suspected of shooting E. One thing he was sure of was that E wouldn't tell shit to the police.

"Naw, brah. That's the crazy part." Pike said unsure. "Don't nobody know who the fuck hit 'em though." That news made BM feel a little more relieved. "Shid that ain't all though." BM waited to hear the rest of the news that he was sure he already knew. "Ike and his cousin got smoked last night. Them niggas went and tried to rob the corner store. Dey say Ike got his face blown off with a pump."

"Damn, that's crazy." BM said nonchalantly.

"You ain't hear 'bout that either?" Pike asked a bit too curious for BM's liking. "Damn, my nigga, what? You been living under a rock fo' the past couple days? You usually keep yo ears to the streets."

"No bullshit." BM falsely agreed. "All this shit happenin' fast though. Aye, but on some real shit, if you get word on who touched my nigga E before I do, please let me know. I'll even pay a fee if I have to 'cause whoeva the nigga is gotta die! ASAP!"

"I already know how you gettin' down, my nigga. I'm surprised you this calm for real." Pike stood to his feet. "Whateva you do, just don't go shootin' up the projects just yet 'cause I'll be right back with yo shit. Give me 'bout twenty minutes or so." He was already walking away before BM could even respond.

"Already. Say no more." BM said anyway. He thought back on the conversation that he had with Pike. Replaying the words over in his head made him think ahead. He knew that the day would come when he would have to face E after his betrayal. Honestly though, he wasn't much worried. He knew that even if E made it through that he would have to take a trip down the Richmond City Jail anyway. And while E sat to fight his charges, BM would have more than enough time to put his next few plans together.

There were four different sections to the Mosby Court Projects. Raven Street, the Top, the Bottom, and the APT's, which was short for Apartments. Or most referred to it as the NO's. The first part of BM's plan was to lay low and grind it out in the bottom of the projects. In order for everything to go accordingly, BM knew that he would need to have plenty of money to make things move. He was a good hustler and always knew how to make a flip. But he never really excelled in his hustle because he was always comfortable with the basics. You know, shoes, clothes, guns, drugs, girls, and a few rental cars. All those things kept his mind distracted from thinking bigger. Now though, he was hungrier than ever. He wanted more. He wanted it all. Even he couldn't explain where this newfound drive was awoken from. Truth be told, it was always there. His hustle was inherited. It was just in him.

Ultimately, BM's objective was to rule. The APT's were a set of one way in and one way out apartments that sat high up on a hill above the projects. Right now, and for the longest, a war is taking place in the APT's. The ongoing battle was between Maines gang and a nigga name Tez's crew. Whatever their odds were, they both had the same thing in mind. And that was to be crowned the king of the hill. Now BM wanted what they had killed and lost loved ones for. Thing was though, the king of the hill's crown could only be worn by someone who was from the top of the projects. BM was from the bottom of Mosby. And the bottom and the top had a history of deadly beef. That went back as far as the project's establishment. Technically, BM had no right to even think about being the king of the hill. If he'd ever even uttered the idea out loud to anyone else, he would be laughed at. Either in his face or behind his back. Either way, the nigga had some nerve. Not only did he have a lot of nerve. The nigga also had balls and a plan. The plan would be quite effective although destructive. BM was about to destroy and rebuild.

***

Only a ten-minute drive down the street, right beneath the cliff of Jefferson Park there was a set of condominiums. Jefferson Park ended with a very sharp cliff. Standing there on the edge of the cliff was a beautiful sight to see. The horizon of a great part of the city was at the disposal of one's eyes. One of the first things that stood out was a set of brand-new condos that was no older than about ten years. Inside the condos, an apartment at the very top, sat a king on his own throne. This throne was undisputed, untouched, and untitled. This king had built his kingdom from the ground up. Leg by leg. One arm at a time. Through all the years of trial and error, his reign was well deserved. Loss after loss, it was a very long time before that had finally arrived.

One. One, two. One, two, three was the rhythm of the knocks at the door. Everyone that occupied the apartment knew exactly who the person on the other side of the door was. One of the goons of the king opened the door and allowed the expected guest to enter. He was trusted and also expected to be armed. So, there was no need for him to be checked and searched for weapons. However, no one ever made it through the threshold without a thorough wire search.

After the guest felt he'd had enough disrespect, he respectfully brushed the hands away from his body. "The fuck off me, nigga!" He spoke. "I ain't no fuckin' snitch!"

The goon guarding the door laughed a little. "Just doin' my job, Keem," he replied. "You know the routine."

"Yeah. I know." Keem confessed. "Yo life gotta suck. Aye, Mac, what's good?" Keem's face lit up as he laid eyes on the man comfortably resting in the chair.

In front of Mac was a floating coffee table. On the table was a chess set where Mac had an intense game going on against himself. Mac looked up from one of his chess pieces on the board at one of his chess pieces in life. "Keem!" He greeted, "My young brotha. What are you lookin' forward to today?" Mac asked Keem one of their everyday questions.

"Today, I'm lookin' forward to opportunity and success at obtainin' it."

"Sounds like a great day to me. I have nothin' but faith that you will receive all the great things that your will works for today."

That was one reason Keem had love and respect for Mac. Damn near all his life he lacked guidance. To have a single person place the least bit of hope into him meant the world to Keem.

"Includin' dis." Mac reached over the right side of the chair and picked up a duffle from a blind spot on the floor.

"Oh shit!" Keem became extra excited, rubbing the palms of his hands together. "That's the two-hundred large?" He wanted to make sure by asking a question he already knew the answer to.

"Naw," Mac denied. The answer made Keem drop the excitement on his face. "It's a quarter," Mac clarified as he tossed the bag on the floor in front of Keem.

"Huh?" Keem was completely confused. He was grateful to receive the extra fifty-thousand dollars. However, Keem was a long shot away from being a fool. He clearly understood that nothing in this world was free. Especially, from a man like Mac. "A quarter million? What's the extras for though?" Keem wisely inquired without sugar coating the question.

Mac leaned up in the chair. "See, that's why I like you, young'in," he said as he made a move on the chess board. "Have a seat," he offered Keem and he was too smart to refuse. "Hey, Chop," Mac called over to one of his goons.

"Yes, sir, boss?" Chop answered.

"Could you bring Keem a drink of his chosen ova, please?"

Chop replied with, "Sure thing, boss."

"The usual," Keem answered before Chop could even muster the question. "You know what it is."

"You're a thinker." Mac continued. He waved an open palm over the chess board, daring Keem to make the next move for the opposite color. Keem took some time to study the pieces positions on the board. Next thing he knew, a move was being made excepting the challenge. "You know why thinkers like other thinkers?" Mac asked as he multitasked between two different chess games.

It was hard for Keem to prioritize right now. His pride and mind were both on the game at hand and the question on his mind. He always loved to answer Mac's questions with accuracy. It gave him a sense of purpose. Plus, he loved the reward like a dog performing the right trick and receiving a treat afterwards. While on the other hand, he would also find great delight in winning the match against his teacher of life. That would prove that he was intellectually making progress in his growth. One thing he noticed was how easy it was for Mac to continue his speech fluidly. And also, keep his thoughts focus on the plan of his game.

"They make them think," Mac answered the question himself once it took Keem too long to think. "Check," Mac said after making his next move. Keem never saw it coming. He used a pawn to block the check. "Thinkers get a rush outta thinking. It's like dopamine is being released from their brains when they do. Providing them with a high that's priceless and enhancing. Or like an orgasm when a genius comes up with a bright idea. Check." This time, Keem used his horse to block the check. "You know?" Mac continued to educate in the school of hard knocks. "Sometimes it's best to move the king around. Even if it's just a spot or two." Mac took his horse and placed it into a new square. "You never wanna box yo king in. Especially, while it's under a threaten attack. Checkmate."

"That's not fair." Keem protested, surprised at the way he noticed that the same pieces that protected him from the prior checks were the same pieces that stopped him from moving out of the current check.

"What's not fair?" Mac wanted to know. "The game of chess or the game of life? Regardless of the circumstances, you have to figure out a way to even out the odds. If not for moment, then definitely for the future. And if you're smart enough it'll take both. That's when you take advantage of things and get ahead. You've done it plenty of times. Even if you were unaware of it." Mac had Keem thinking hard as he deeply pondered on the meaning of his words. "When you came into the womb of yo mother, the odds were against you. One to a million when your pops busted that nut. And out of all of them seeds, you was the one that wiggled through the oval. You follow me?"

41

Keem simply nodded. Like Hov said in that one song, he was like a dog that didn't speak but he understood. He never in life thought about the odds of the many seeds that had swam through his mother's pussy and him being the only one to make it out. It made him feel special as if he was here for a special purpose. Something divine. Keem lifted his glass and took a sip of the D'ussé that sat in the glass as Mac continued to talk.

Noticing the complexed look on Keem's face, Mac knew it was time to drive the screw home. "Of course, as we discussed, the two-hundred thousand was for the hit. The price was so high because I understand the love that was expressed between the two of you. I imagine that it must have been a difficult job. But you were the best person for it. You brought him in, you take him out. Plus, you would be the least person expected. Ace was a good soulja indeed. But law 1 in 48 Laws of Power: Never Outshine The Master. Ace became big headed and sloppy. The decisions and moves he started to make could have had the whole team toppled.

"Now an extra fifty thousand is due because of a simple request that I have from you. It's my son." Just at the thought of having to deal with Mac's son pissed Keem off silently. "Word came to me this morning before the sun could even show its face that he may find himself in a handful of trouble soon. Seems as if he's bitten off more than he may be able to chew."

"Uh huh," Keem simply said, still following along with Mac's words.

"I need you to keep watch on him. Follow his moves. See what he may be up to."

"What? So, you want me to sit around all day and follow that nigga around for fifty thousand dollars? I would've been made that within the next few hours or so, Mac. I'on even babysit my own daughter."

"I want you to go through every now and then to see for yo self, with yo own eyes what he's doin'. What I really meant by watch was to get one of your lil' troops or somethin' on him. Not twenty-four-seven. But at least the majority of the day for the next few months. Every month I'll provide you with another fifty to keep whoeva you decide to hire for the job happy. Do we have an agreement?"

"Ight, that's a bet, Mac. Sounds like a plan, boss. I'ma get one of my young'ins on it."

"I had no doubt that you would," Mac admitted, picking up a glass of his favorite drink. "Ayee, this is to the next level." He offered a toast.

Keem raised his glass and clanked it against Mac's "To the next level indeed." He agreed.

LESSON 1.6
Never Snitch

A few hours later and a few miles away was the VCU/MCV hospital. Not too long out of an emergency surgery, well on his way to recovery, E laid up in a hospital bed. Shot five times, he was lucky to survive the attack. Only two bullets really threatened his life. One coming within an inch of his heart. The doctors were successful at the removal of the bullet. Another one had skidded the left side of his body. It would have been just a flesh wound except for the bullet tapping a rib that fractured it. Another bullet had traveled right above E's heart, barely missing the main artery that sat above it.

E was pissed off like never before. Hurt beyond measures. For some reason, he knew that he could trust BM with a million dollars. It hurt to realize that he was wrong. His mind raced like legs at a track meet. Like why the fuck would BM do some shit like that to him? He wanted to believe that it was because of the money. Exactly how much money was it, he wondered. A thousand or two. Maybe a few. That's it? It really tormented E's heart with hurt to think that BM carried ill will towards him the whole time. E would've did a life sentence for that nigga. Shit, he would have sacrificed his life for that nigga. On just them thoughts alone, it forced E to drift into the memories that he tried with all his strength to avoid.

***

"I swear that nigga be actin' like he wants smoke with a nigga, fool." The flash back was a memory into the year of the 2016 summer. On Redd Street in Mosby Court Projects. BM, the older of the two by a few months, referred to E. The person he spoke of was a fourteen year young'in that went by the handle Slay.

Slay was well respected by not only his peers, but the generations before him as well. At thirteen, he had gained his reputation and respect by catching the murderer of a twenty-two years of age Mosby veteran. Not only had he murdered with the heart of a savage, but when he was arrested as a juvenile, he remained as silent as a mime. Once he touched down, after beating the murder wrap due to a lack of evidence, he was more respected than most niggas twice his age. In addition to respect was fear. Slay allowed them both to go straight to his head. He started to feel like Mr. Untouchable, as if the same thing couldn't happen to him.

"That nigga ain't thinkin' 'bout you, my nigga." E tried to convince his friend. "Plus, I'm tellin' you, on gang, if he try some fuck shit I'ma blow his dumb ass." Underneath E's shirt was a .38 revolver. But no one knew it but him.

"Nigga, with what?" BM asked, practically taking his friend as a mere joke. "We ain't even got the first scrap."

"Shid..." E laughed, amused at how slimy he was able to move without being expected as a threat. "Follow me right quick." Together they exited the curb and left the scene, traveling to a cut behind one of the project buildings. E led; BM followed. E turned around and faced BM once he felt that all eyes were off him. He lifted his shirt and exposed the handle of the concealed firearm.

"Oh shit, nigga!" BM grew excited. "Why the fuck you ain't put me on game, bitch?" he asked anxiously.

"'Cause, fool, niggas don't need to know we totin'. I swear to God, if a nigga move foolish, I'ma slime a nigga out like a splat gun. That's on my mama."

"Let me see that joint, brah?" BM went to reach.

E quickly pulled his shirt back down and took a step back away from BM. "Naw, brah," E denied the request. "I know you, brah. You gone make shit hot. That ain't what we need. It's best to stay the underdog. You feel me? That way we can rock a nigga to sleep. Let 'em act stupid, then we can put a nigga to sleep for eternity."

Little did E know that was the first taste of bad blood between the two. Even though it was only a drip, the taste was strong enough to fuel the envy that was planted in BM's heart. From there it started to grow. Although E was right and had a good point, BM didn't like the fact that he had to take the position of following the leader.

"Ight, my nigga. All I know is one thing. You better bomb that mafucka! Our life in yo hands."

Technically, at this point, neither of the young'ins had proved that they had the balls to pull the trigger. It didn't bother E as much. But BM wanted to prove that point as if his life depended on it.

"On my dead mama, nigga. You ain't sayin' shit."

They walked back to the scene where plenty of criminal activities took place.

"Aye Tisha, what's up, shawty?" BM called out to one of his neighborhood crushes. He spotted her as soon as he revealed himself from the project cut

Only thirteen, Tisha dressed as if she was twenty-three. In the scorching summer heat, she wore short shorts that exposed her immature cheeks, and a fresh wife beater with no bra on her full breast. "Hey... BM!" Tisha song in response. Sounding as happy as ever.

"You know what's going on. A nigga tryna bust that cherry," BM said approaching her with his crotch in his hand. Truth be told, BM was still a virgin himself.

"Boy, you betta stop playin'." She advised with a laugh. "You know you my nigga and shit, but you must don't know—"

"Ayee, my nigga! You need to back up off my bitch 'for it be a mafuckin' problem!" Slay was approaching the two from across the street.

BM stood stuck with a dumbfounded look on his face. Slay shoved Tisha slightly backwards and stepped in between her and BM. What BM didn't know was that Tisha was no longer a virgin. And worst news to his ears, she now belonged to Slay who was the same person who broke her virginity.

"I see you been flirtin' with my lil' shawty for a minute now." Slay locked eye contact with BM. "What you slow or somethin'? You don't know what the fuck goin' on? 'Cause if you do, you damn sure actin' like you don't give a fuck, when I suggest that you definitely should."

BM never knew what heartbreak felt like. At that moment though, that's exactly what he thought he was going through. It was either that, or the embarrassment of the way Slay had pulled up on him in front of everyone that stood on Redd Street. "Nigga, ain't nobody trippin' 'bout no bitch, nigga!" BM felt as if he had to stand his ground. "I'on know what the fuck you think this is but—"

Just the fact of him knowing that E and him had the tool, gave a little boost to BM's heart. But still though, he'd have to get to it first. It wasn't even a question if Slay was strapped or not. To even ask the question would be like a slap in the face. With that fact alone, Slay could give two fucks about all that raw-raw shit. He never did and definitely didn't at that moment.

"Lil' nigga what you tryna do? Straight up. I'on like yo ass anyway. How the hell yo ass a virgin and still smell like pussy? Out cha cappin' like you fuckin' shit." A few people that stood by and watched the altercation go down laughed. Slay was not trying to be funny though. He was dead ass serious. He had stepped so close to BM's face that if the wind blew, it would cause one of Slay's dreads to fly right into the face of BM.

"Nigga you better get the fuck out my face." BM desperately wished that he had that gun on him right then at that moment. He knew that if he did, the conversation would be over. There would be nothing else to talk about because he would have made sure that Slay wouldn't be able to talk at all.

"Or what, pussy?" The last thing that came out of Slay's mouth was followed by a sprinkle of saliva.

With that it was enough said. Forcefully, BM had pushed Slay in his chest causing him to stumble back a couple steps. Before Slay could even react, people were already ducking and running wisely getting out of the way.

The push only did two things at the most. Piss Slay off even more than he already was, and it gave him just enough room to pull the Glock .17 with the slightly extended clip under his Nike *Just Do It* shirt. He whipped it out and aimed it up. All BM could do was stare down the hole of the barrel. Slay said, followed by a light laugh, "You really look like a pussy with the dick in yo face." BM said nothing. What could he say? With this mini psycho on the other side of the gun, it was if he was already dead. "Looks like you already know what time it is. Time to say goodnight, bitch!"

Boom! The single shot echoed throughout the thick tension in the air, cutting it thin like a knife to a slice of bologna. Damn near everyone was in shock as if they've never witnessed a shooting before. As if it was something that was impossible to happen. Blood was splattered and had begun to drip down BM's face. Now he looked three times as dumb as he did before.

Slay never seen it coming. No one did for that matter. Except for the person who waited for it to happen. For BM, it seemed as if it took forever. But it worked out perfectly. Inch by inch, creeping the few feet to close the distance between him and his target, E stealthy made his way towards Slay's backside. He knew he couldn't play. Like BM had said earlier, their lives were in E's hand. The shit damn near felt like a jinx. E was smart. He knew that Slay was more experienced. And that he had at least twenty more shots to spare. The only advantages that E had on his side was being counted out, along with the element of surprise. Together, they were deadly combinations. All he needed was the heart to capitalize.

Slay's body dropped in front of BM like the wrong block being pulled out of a Jenga game. BM felt powerful as ever watching his enemy fall to his feet, covering the ground like the dirt he came from.

Coming to their realization that Slay was just murdered in cold blood, the projects went crazy. "Oh my God!" Tisha screamed. "What did you do?" Her heart had dropped. She screamed so loud that it felt like her lungs collapsed. She dropped to her knees beside Slay and checked to see if her eyes were playing tricks on her. She wanted to see if it was real. That Slay was really dead.

"Come on, brah. We gotta go." E tugged on the tail of BM's shirt. "We gotta get the fuck outta here."

BM barely budged. He stood there in a daze watching Tisha cry over Slay. At that moment, BM's energy shifted to a dark place. This was some powerful shit he was witnessing. The will to take a man's life was now something he longed for. Not pussy. Not money. Not love. Not drugs. But murder. At twelve years old, all BM wanted was to murder. And that's where the second drop of bad blood in his mouth for E came from. It was jealousy. Despite the fact that E had just saved his life BM envied the fact that E was the first one to get his hands covered in blood. For the years that came after, BM dropped body after body in a quiet competition with his teammate, making sure to always stay up on the count. No matter how many he killed though, it was always that first one that was put on the map. The one that saved BM's life.

E was known forever as the loyal, bravehearted hero that slayed the hood's slayer. And boy did BM hate it with a deep passion.

"BM!" E shouted. "Fuck, my nigga! Let's fuckin' go!" Sirens were on their way. He was relieved as hell when BM came back to his senses. Together, like they did everything, BM and E fled the scene, mazing their way back to the bottom of the projects which was their neck of the woods.

About a handful of days later, the police received a tip that BM and E may have been the two behind the murder of Slay. They scooped the little niggas up and tried to crack them at the police station with heavy interrogations.

Pulling all the tricks out the bag, they offered food and sodas. Neither of the boys took even a sip of water. The police tried the good cop and bad cop thing. But the pair treated the police both the same. Replying with mostly silence or the words 'I don't know,' and a lot of 'fuck yous.' They sent threats of life sentences from being charged as adults. Them little niggas didn't give a fuck still though. As long as they could do the time together, they weren't tripping one bit, mostly because they were pissed off that the young gangsters were golden solid and having nothing to do with having the proper evidence. The police charged them with first degree murder and locked them away in the juvenile detention center. Due to the fact that it was one shot, they both couldn't be found guilty of the same charge. The state had no evidence. And no witness. A couple months later the case was forced to be dismissed.

BM and E had touched down untouched. Just in time to catch the last few weeks of the summer. It was lit for them. They were hood legends in the walking flesh. From there, they added to their legacy. Not a whole gang. Just the two of them. Together or apart, they were not to be fucked with.

***

"Mr. E'Vel Foster. I'm pretty sure you're aware of who I am already." Detective Calvez said as he entered the room. The entrance of the man broke E out of his memory bank. "Therefore, we could cut straight to the chase. I know your rap sheet. I know your MO. Only difference is I'm used to chasing you around. This would be the first time I'd ever had to chase down a suspect for you though."

"You ain't gotta do shit for me," E said, honestly meaning it.

"Come on, Foster. I'm just here to do my job."

"Well do it den. I ain't stoppin' you. And I damn sure ain't gone help yo ass."

"Okay. Well, I guess for the sake of doing my job, do you know who shot you?"

"What?" E asked looking confused as ever. "I got shot?" He made sure that he made his surprised tone seem believable.

Detective Calvez released a sigh of frustration. "Yes, you were shot, Foster." He reminded E of what he obviously already knew.

"Hell naw!" E nonchalantly answered with a slight hint of shock still. "All I know is I woke up like dis."

"Okay. So, were you aware that we found you unconscious with drugs and a firearm within a few feet of your person?"

When BM had shot him, E knew that his best bet was to play dead. He even knew what BM was up to when he took the money and recreational drugs from his pockets and left the crack cocaine and gun. They had used that trick plenty of times in order to throw off the police's crime scene. Once BM had left out the back door, E used the rest of the strength that he had in his body to get the gun and drugs off him. He threw them as far away from himself as he possibly could. Aiming them towards the back door. Once that was done, he laid there and awaited rescue while drifting in and out of consciousness.

"How the hell is I'm supposed to know that if I was unconscious?" E asked a question so good that even made the detective feel dumb. "And I'on gives a fuck what you say you found. Wasn't none of that shit mine. So, I ain't even tryna hear that shit."

"Okay, Foster. That's the game you want to play. We'll see what song you'll be signing when it all comes falling down on you." Detective Calvez turned around and headed towards the door with a folder tucked underneath his armpit. "Now he's not talking. I knew he wouldn't though." Calvez said on the other side of the closed door.

"You want me to go in and give it a shot?" Winchester replied.

"No need to. He's a solid kid. The type that makes us work. Been like that his whole life. I think the best thing to do now is to follow Macsby. He may take us straight to the shooter while looking for retaliation." The detectives made their way down the hall.

E laid up in the hospital bed with an evil grin that stretched from ear to ear. "I ain't no ma'fuckin' snitch," he mumbled to himself. "Bitch ass nigga got me fucked up." E grabbed the remote to the TV. "I'on even know why that fool came at me like that. Ma'fucka already know what the count is." While flicking through the channels, he really paid no attention to what was being broadcast. All he thought about was the day he would be able to lay his eyes on BM again. The cling from the handcuffs on his wrist reminded him that he'd have to go through the system. But that only gave him more time to plot an evil scheme.

LESSON 1.7
Cheaters Never Win… For Now

"You better not answer that ma'fuckin' phone," Tank said in a minor threat. He was laying on his back on the bed butt ass naked, underneath a light brown, caramel complexion baddie. He looked up at her pretty perky titties as they bounced precisely.

"Shut the fuck up, nigga!" The gorgeous woman named Kimberly replied. She used both hands to cover Tank's mouth to assure his silence. As she rode his dick, she felt the head of it barely touching her spot. The phone continued to ring. She continued to ignore it. Leaving one hand still covering Tank's mouth, she took the other hand and wrapped it around his throat. She wasn't trying to hurt him. At least, not that much. She just wanted to motivate him to push a little harder. "Fuck me, nigga! You better fuck this pussy! Harder!" She begged urgently.

Tank wrapped his hands around the backside of Kimberly, gripping both of her ass cheeks. He lifted them up and thrusted forcefully from the bottom. Kimberly had a small frame but was thick in all the right places. Tank was almost twice her size. As he pumped over and over, Kimberly felt as if the dick had reached her spine. Even if not, it had definitely touched her spot with every stroke. "Dis how you want it? You want dis dick like dis?" Tank questioned full of aggression and lust.

"Yes! Like that. Just like that!" With the hand that had kept his mouth closed, Kimberly now used to reach back to juggle and pull on Tank's nut sack. It drove him crazy when she played with his balls every time. Kimberly's phone had finally stopped ringing. Literally five seconds later, it had started to ring again. It's been doing that none-stop for about the last three minutes. You would think that the sound of ringing would get on one's nerve during sex. Not for Kimberly though. In some sick way, that only she could explain, it actually made her hornier. She thrived off the guilty pleasure.

"Aww… shit!" Tank moaned a warning of a nut that was on the way.

"No. No. No, please! Wait for me, please." Kimberly begged. "Oh my God! It feels so fuckin' good. I'm-I'm-com… inga!" Simultaneously, they exploded in pleasure from the elevation of lust. Kimberly laid on Tank's chest for a rest to catch her breath. Her phone began a new set of rings. She reached over to grab it. Kimberly took a look at her phone to see who it was that was blowing her line up so eagerly even though she already knew. Just as she expected, it was Derek.

"Damn you got that nigga wide open, don't you?" Tank asked in a tease.

"Shut up, boy." Kimberly giggled. "Like you ain't got the thirst for these juices."

"You know that shit fire." Tank laughed along as he laid a heavy smack on one of her ass cheeks with his bear claw-like hand.

"Damn, boy," she said still in pain. "I told you to stop doin' that shit." Another set of rings came blasting through the phone. "You better not say a ma'thafuckin' word." She sat up preparing to answer the phone. "Hello."

"Damn! Where the fuck you at?" It was so quiet that Tank could hear the angry voice of Derek over the phone.

"Ohh…" Tank said very silently with a balled-up fist over the smile on his face.

Kimberly placed her index finger over her lips, indicating for Tank to remain quiet. "I'm right here on the Exxon on Nine Mile Road, Boo. I was in the store and left my phone in the car." Kimberly lied like a true professional. "And why the fuck you yellin' and all that?"

"'Cause, I been callin' yo phone for some shit. You know a nigga gotta go to work and you makin' me late, *again!*"

"Ight, calm down, damn. I'm on my way." Kimberly was getting pissed off. Not at Derek though because he had a vital point. It was Tank that was making her feel some type of way. He found it humorous to wiggle two fingers inside of her pussy while his thumb rotated around her clitoris. The hand action was making both of them horny all over again. Kimberly was loving the feeling so much that she started to whine on Tank's fingers. Her pussy was so soaking wet that it left his fingers moist and creamy.

"For real, mane. Hurry the fuck up. You startin' to piss me off with this shit." Derek was from the streets but not necessarily stamped a street a nigga. He'd rather work his way into the bag. Couldn't say the same for his high school sweetheart though. She was as street as the material that made them. Never had a job and not even willing to work one. Every dollar she made came directly off the land.

"Ight, Boo. I'm comin' now, damn. Now can I get off this phone so I can listen to my music while I drive, please?" Derek didn't even bother to reply. All he did was hang the phone up. "He gets on my fuckin' nerves." Kimberly expressed herself verbally.

"I'ma be real though." Tank spoke up. "If you was my bitch, I'll be on yo ass, too."

"You still be on my ass." Kimberly just knew she was that bitch. Aside from her morals and principles though, she was. Her skin was like cocoa smooth and soft. It glowed as if she was fresh out of prison. Her eyes were seductive, eyebrows were thick but stayed arched. Eyelashes were long and full. That was all natural. It only intensified when she dolled herself up. "It's a good thing I ain't yo bitch anyway. You would've been killed a bitch." Tank laughed at the comment knowing that it was probably true, due to the games that she played. "Speakin' of yo bitch. Where the hell she at anyway?"

"Shid, I'on know. Probably out doin' the same shit you doin'," Tank replied.

"What?" Kimberly asked, shocked. "You think she'll play with you like that?"

"I mean I'm pretty sure it's an eighty percent chance that she knows what the hell I be up to. So, I wouldn't put nothin' past her ass."

"Y'all niggas ain't shit." Kimberly said.

"Y'all bitches worse than niggas." Tank shot back.

"How you gone say that when you sittin' in that girl house fuckin' another woman in her bed?"

"What?" *Kimberly had the nerve*, Tank thought. "How you gone say that when you the bitch I'm fuckin'? And you know what's goin' on. It ain't like you in the dark about it."

"I'm just sayin'. And plus, you ain't my nigga, so."

"Oh, so you think yo nigga ain't out here doin' the same shit?"

"Hell naw!" Kimberly actually said that with one-hundred percent assurance. "Derek ain't no dog. I got a good man."

"And yet you still treat 'em like a dog. Like I said, y'all bitches worse than niggas."

"But you may have a good girl and you still dog her out."

"For one, I don't know that for sure. Plus, I'm a dog." Tank admitted shamelessly.

"You ain't shit."

"Guess we a good match 'cause that makes both of us." Tank agreed.

"Whateva. Look, I gotta go." Kimberly said. She leaned down and placed a kiss on Tank's lips.

"Carry yo ass then." Tank dismissed. "You know the vibes. Backdoor action."

"You ain't gone see me out?"

"Yeah, I gotta lock the door anyway."

Kimberly threw her clothes on. Before heading out the door, she stopped at the bathroom. In her bag were some tampons and a bottle of fake blood. You know the kind that a vampire may use on Halloween or something. She squeezed a good amount of the synthetic blood into the pad, then placed it in her panties before pulling them up. Just an old trick she used from time to time. One that Derek somehow always foolishly fell for. Tank waited for her to come out of the bathroom. Once she finally did, he walked to the backdoor of the apartment. She walked through the back of the projects in Fair Field Court. Heading towards 27th Street, she hopped in her car and pulled off.

Tank and Kimberly thought that they were being wise by using the backdoor to sneak out of the apartment. What they didn't realize, though, was that there was definitely a set of eyes watching them. "Umm-hmm, bitch, you are fuckin' right." Kadesha said over the phone to her friend, Shawndra. "I can't believe this nigga had the nerve to bring a bitch in yo fuckin' crib though. Like, I'm hot-hot. What the fuck you tryna do, 'cause we can stomp this bitch to the concrete right now." Kadesha was dead serious.

"Naw." Shawndra said parked in the front of her apartment on Rosetta Street. "We gone catch her later 'cause if we do it now, it's gone put this lame ass nigga on game that we hip to him. And he the one that I really want. For now, just follow the bitch and see where she goes. I'ma go in here and play my role with this dummy. Shoot me a text when she gets to where she goin'."

"Ight, I got you." Kadesha promised. She hung up the phone and followed behind Kimberly at a nice distance.

The travel was short; about a five-minute drive from Fair Field to Whitcomb Court. Kimberly parked on Ambrose Street and Kadesha parked a few cars down from her. Picking up her phone, Kadesha texted Shawndra, telling her to call her now. Ten seconds later, her phone was ringing. "Hello." Kadesha answered.

"Yeah, what's up girl? Y'all stopped already?" Shawndra asked a couple questions.

"Hell yeah. If I ain't mistaken, the bitch lives in Whitcomb 'cause that's where she stopped at. We right here on Ambrose now. She already went in the house. I'ma sit right here to see how long she will stay. You okay?" Kadesha had to check on her best friend.

"Yeah girl. I'm okay. It's takin' everything in a bitch, though, not to stab the fuck out this clown ass, disloyal ass nigga. Do you know it smell like straight pussy, balls, and ass all in my room? I couldn't even stand to stay in there."

"Damn, Bestie. That's some fucked up shit. I swear you either a strong bitch or a mafuckin' fool. What the hell that nigga doin' anyway?"

"He in the shower right now."

"And what you doin'?" Kadesha was always nosey. Shawndra was used to it.

"Fixin' his ass somethin' to eat."

"What? Bitch!" Kadesha asked half-surprised and half-disappointed. "You's a good one. That nigga must got some goat dick. Unless you 'bout to put some poison in the nigga shit or somethin'."

"The dick is good, but not worth the heartbreak. I'm sick to my stomach of how this nigga keep playin' me. And, no I'm not gone poison him, fool. That shit gone come right back to me."

"Well, bitch, we need to do somethin' 'bout his ass."

"I know that, hoe. But if I say somethin', he ain't gone do shit but beat my mafuckin' ass again. I wish my fuckin' brother was home, shawty, for real."

"No bullshit. Aye, but listen though. It's a nigga comin' out the apartment that she just went into. Look like he got on a work uniform. Hold on." Kadesha put the phone on speaker, placed it in her cup holder, and shifted the gear of the car into drive. Slowly she rode down the street. "Yep girl. The nigga work at DTLR somewhere." The tint was five percent on her Lexus. No way that the two being spied on would be able to see the person inside the car. "Oh yeah, this gotta be her apartment. She standin' in the screen door holdin' a baby. And they arguin', bitch." Kadesha rolled the window down, but only enough to allow the words being yelled to leak into the car.

"I swear to God!" Kimberly yelled from the porch over her crying baby. "I can't wait to get my own car!"

"How the fuck you mad 'cause I gotta go to work?" Derek asked, making his way to the driver's car door.

"'Cause you actin' funny. Like I can't drop yo ass off at work."

"Fuck naw." Derek opened the car door. "I'm not gone keep waistin' money on an Uber 'cause yo ass always think it's cool to pick a nigga up from work late and shit." Derek hopped in his car and slammed the door.

"Ooohhh…" Kadesha said, loving the action. "That nigga is mad-mad. He sexy too though." She threw in. Kadesha traveled a few feet further down the street again and parked. "I wanna see what store he works at."

"Girl, you ain't got nothin' else better to do? I told yo ass to see where she go to. Not stalk her whole family."

"Shid, you never know. This shit might come in handy one day." Kadesha allowed for Derek's black Nissan truck to roll past her. She waited until he broke at the stop sign and continued with a left turn on Sussex Street, before she decided to follow. Another left turn on Whitcomb Street. Then another on Mechanicsville. "Damn, this nigga drivin' like he at the Richmond Raceway."

"Girl, he probably noticed yo crazy ass followin' him." Shawndra uttered in a panic.

"Hell, naw girl, his ass just got road rage. I told you he was mad before he got into the car." With the speed that Derek was putting on the meter, it didn't take long at all for him to reach his workplace. "Oh, he work right down the street at the shoppin' center on Mechanicsville."

"Bitch don't let him see you!" Shawndra demanded.

"I'm not. I ain't gone even turn in there."

"You my bitch for sho though."

"You already know I got your back. But for real though, we need to come up with a plan. Gotta make this nigga pay for the way he been treatin' you. Yo ass ain't cheated on that nigga not once. But you keep on takin' this shit. I just don't get it."

"Everything gone workout," Shawndra said hopefully. "We just gotta be smart 'bout the way we move. Look bitch, he out the shower. I gotta go. Love you."

"Love you too, girl." They hung up their phones.

LESSON 1.8
Be Aware of Your Surroundings

Keem sat in the heart of the projects that he grew up in which was Hill Side Court. He was parked in a rental with another one right behind him. He waited for his target to pop up on the scene as he did just about every day.

"I'on know why you just don't let me do that shit, brah." Shy asked his big brother from the passenger seat. "I can handle it."

"'Cause, brah, dude ass crazy for real. And I value yo life too much just to throw you out into the field on a fuckin' dummy mission," Keem said truthfully. The only reason Shy was even in the car at the time was because he needed someone to operate the rental that was parked behind him. Now that the cars were in the position that Keem needed them to be in, he no longer needed his little brother. For the last eighteen minutes, he had tried to put Shy out of the car.

"Brah, I'm tellin' you now. You 'bout to pay them lil' niggas all that money and they ain't gone do shit but trick the whole mission up."

"I'on know lil' brah. It sounds like you hatin' a lil' bit if you ask me." Keem was strolling down his Instagram page. It was something for him to do while he waited and indulged in the small conversation with Shy. "I know one thing though. I hope these lil' niggas hurry up. You don't have one of they numbers?" Keem looked over to ask Shy.

"Nope." Shy quickly lied arrogantly with a splash of nonchalance.

"You lyin ma'fucka. Get the fuck out my car." There was no real threat behind Keem's demand. He hated to treat his baby brother like a kid. But the fact that they had already lost a brother to the streets caused Keem to cover Shy with shelter.

Wild Boy was the middle son between Keem and Shy. If he'd still been alive, he would have been twenty-four years old. Wild Boy was only twenty years of age when he was murdered. That was four years ago. The same number of years that Keem had lived with the regret of his passing brother. Keem led as if Wild Boy's death was his fault because he had welcomed Wild Boy into the streets with open arms. But then again, Wild Boy wouldn't be denied. Shy and Wild Boy were the total opposites. Shy was smart and played it low key while Wild Boy was hot headed and loved to be seen. No matter how much potential Keem saw in Shy, he just wouldn't allow Shy to make a name for himself in the streets. Although, deep down inside, he would definitely respect it if Shy decided to take it.

"Der go yo lil' flunkies right there." Shy announced dryly.

"How you sittin' right here beggin' to be a flunky? But you gone talk shit 'bout them?" Keem didn't really care for Shy's answer. He honked the horn of the car trying to get the attention of the two boys.

"It ain't what you do." Shy spoke. "It's how you do it." Both Shy and Keem looked from behind the tint of the car. They shared a laugh when they saw the young boys duck and reach for their weapons. "Them niggas scared as a bitch." Shy chuckled.

"They better not up at this car." Keem laughed but was dead ass serious. "I know that much."

"Maine, them niggas 'bout to run. You talkin' 'bout shootin'." Shy was weak to his stomach from laughter.

"Let the window down, brah." Keem ordered Shy.

"Aye!" Shy yelled out the window after doing what he was told. "Y'all niggas stop actin' like y'all got opps out here. Ain't nobody thinkin' 'bout y'all niggas." Keem laughed at his lil' brother's comment.

"Ayee, Shy!" A short young'in at the age of seventeen yelled back. He was relieved as hell when he saw the face of someone who didn't mean any harm. "Y'all niggas stop playin' for real!" Lil' One shouted out.

"Y'all niggas wasn't gone do shit. Soft ass niggas was 'bout to haul ass," Shy said as he and Keem continued to laugh.

"Shid... we thought y'all niggas was twelve for real." The older young'in said. He was black as tar and tall. They called him Crow.

"Tell them lil' niggas get in the car." Keem told Shy and Shy sent the order. The two young'ins followed the demand.

"Oh shit!" Lil' One was excited as he climbed into the back seat of the car with Crow jumping in right behind him. "What's up Keem? I ain't know you was in this bitch." Keem was a living legend to the residents of Hill Side Court. Similar to BG out New Orleans.

"You never know when I might pop out, Lil' One. What's up, Crow?"

"What's good, Keem? I ain't on shit. Out this bitch tryna get like you, my nigga." Crow replied.

"Shid... I might have a way for y'all fools to kick in the door. That's if y'all can handle the situation. I ain't gone lie, lil' brah right here don't think y'all got it in y'all." Keem looked over to Shy with a sly smirk on his face.

"Say no more, fool." Crow was anxious. He knew, like Lil' One, that anything dealing with Keem was big. Especially, being that he came looking for them. Usually, it was the other way around.

"Yeah. Just let us know what the mission is." Lil' One chipped in.

"Already." Keem said. "Listen up. I'm only gone say this once. I got a rental right behind us. I'ma let y'all hold it down for as long as needed. We might even switch it up every now and den. One trick up and it's ova with. But that ain't even the sweet part. Here's where it gets excitin'. Everyday y'all niggas on the mission, I'ma pay y'all a band. That's five hundred dollars apiece every day. In a month, y'all niggas could be up fifteen bands each. At least ten. If y'all can't come up off that, y'all dicks deserve to be in the dirt. Pause."

"Ight but you still ain't tell us what we gotta do yet." Crow said.

"Shid... I'on give a fuck what we gotta do. I'm down!" Lil' One was always hyperactive. But the thought of him coming up on some bands had him exhilarated.

"That's what the fuck I'm talkin' 'bout." Keem was happy to hear. "Give them lil' niggas the key and the phone," he told Shy. "That's the keys to the rental. Don't argue too soon ova who gone be the driver. Y'all niggas gone have some long shifts. Therefore, it'll be enough time for both of y'all to be behind the wheel. Just can't get on no hot shit. I'on give a fuck what y'all do with y'all phones. But the phones I just gave y'all, it has one number in it. That's the number to the burner on this end. Do not call anybody else from that number. When I text you and say, 'fade away,' that means to dispose of that mafucka ASAP. And meet me or Shy back round here at this same spot. Got it?" Keem looked at the boys' eyes through the rearview mirrors. They were all ears.

"Got it, big dawg." Lil' One replied.

"Already." Agreed Crow.

"Ight, bet. Hop in the rental and follow us."

They followed Keem's orders and exited the vehicle. Keem waited for the barely legal teenagers to get into the other car before pulling off. Shy was happy just to still be in the car with Keem. Although he was humbled soul, it still baffled him that his brother would rather pay thousands of dollars to someone outside his bloodline instead of keeping the money in the family. It just made no sense to him. Verbally, he remained silent. But his thoughts were loud and clear.

"You know I gotta bigga plan for you, right?" Keem asked. The question kind of shocked Shy. It's like Keem had just read his mind. "It's called longevity." Shy knew something was up because Keem was doing something that he never did. He rode in silence without the blast of music pumping through his speakers. "See, time is money." Keem continued as he filled the silence with his words. "It takes time to make money. You follow me?" Shy replied with the nod of his head. "At other times, you can spend money to buy time. Understand?" he asked, trying not to lose Shy in the essence of time.

"Yeah, I get all that," Shy answered before asking, "but where you goin' with all dis?"

"That's what I'm doin' with these lil' niggas." Keem admitted. "I'm just buyin' their time so I can spend mine on doin' bigga and betta things. See, someone paid me to do a job. Fifty thousand. I took twenty off the top. Paid myself first and hired two dummies with nothin' but time on their hands to do the job for me. You feel me?" Shy silently had to admit the way Keem spent the money did make sense, now that he thought about it the way a boss would. "Now tell me this Shy, why in the hell would I pay you to do a fool's job when you could be doing somethin' bigga and betta with yo time? Somethin' that could secure yo future?"

"What could secure my future betta then money?" Shy asked a pretty good question.

"Gainin' the intelligence on what to with it once you get it." Keem shot back with a quick witty answer. After that, there was no more left to say. Keem turned the music up and let sound waves of Est Gee and Jeezy *Da Realest* bump through the speakers as he hopped on the highway heading north of Richmond.

A few songs later, they had made it to their destination. After driving through the hood a couple of times, Keem had spotted their target. "Der that lil' nigga go right there." Keem announced. "I'on know why that lil' nigga was so hard to find today. He usually the main one on the scene out this bitch. He must be on some layin' low type shit." Keem pulled over and parked at the end of the block. It was a half of block away from the person they watched. Close enough to see him. But far away to not be directly detected.

"Who the fuck is dude?" Shy was curious as he studied the man that appeared to be around the same age as him. He paid extra attention to every detail about the target. How he made his plays as the drug addicts came back-to-back. How he treated them. The alley he stood in. The trash can he hid his pack under. The screen door he swung open and close. Even how many times he checked his phone in the matter of minutes that they watched him.

"That's Mac's son. Baby Mac." Keem explained. "They call him BM out here. The lil' nigga hates to be associated with his pops. Let's just say, a whole lot of penitentiary time could break a family's bond to the point of no return. Anyway, the lil' nigga posed to be in some shit. If you ask me though, it looks like he gettin' on his shit."

"Naw, I heard of dude befo'. He be thuggin' with E from out here. Them niggas' names be ringin' bells."

"Yeah, I know. Another reason why I'on want you to have nothin' to do with this shit. I know you got my blood runnin' all through you. But that would be like throwin' you to the wolves with no justification. Besides, I fuck with the way them lil' niggas handle they business. At the end of day though, it's all business. And one business I'll never intervene with is family business. Another reason why yo thirsty ass stayin' out this shit. You feel me?"

"Yeah, I feel you. Now that you put it like that."

"Let me see that phone." Shy handed Keem the burner. Keem dialed the only number that was stored in the contacts.

"Yo," Lil' One answered the phone, sitting in the passenger side of the rental car.

"Put me on speaker," Keem ordered through the speaker of the burner he held in his hand.

"Ight, hold on." Lil' One paused. "Ight, you good. Go head."

"Y'all see that nigga in the alley?" Keem asked both of the young'ins through the speaker phone. "The only one that don't look like a junky cacthin' all the plays."

"Yeah," Crow replied. "That's BM. We know that nigga."

"Yeah, he done came out to Hill Side a few times." Lil' one confessed. "And he used to go to CCP with us a couple years back. Dude be piped up. Him and that nigga E." Keem and Shy looked over at each other but remained silent. "What the hell you want us to do with brah? Kill him or somethin'?"

"Naw." Keem chuckled lightly. "Don't kill him. Just watch him."

"Watch 'em?" Lil' One and Crow asked in a union of confusion. "You mean like steak out or somethin'?" Lil' One added.

"Yeah, I guess somethin' like that. What, y'all not down fo' the mission no more? If not, just let me know. I know somebody that's dyin' to take the position." Keem cut his eye over at Shy with a smile on his face.

"Naw, we got dis." Crow spoke for the both of them.

"Yeah, we got dis." Lil' one agreed. "But for how long though?"

"For a thousand dollars a day," Keem replied sarcastically. "Naw, for real though. I really don't know. It may be a day. It may be a month. It may be three days. It may be three months. Just check in with me every now and den. And let me know what the nigga routine lookin' like. Or if something out of the ordinary happens. I'll hit y'all every once in a while for a report and shit like that. Got it?"

"Yeah, but what 'bout…?"

"Look in the armrest." Keem cut the question off that was on its way to him.

Lil' One lifted the armrest and laid his eyes on the ten hundred dollar bills that lay there. "Oh, ight bet." Was all he had to say.

"That's the payment for today. Y'all got it from here?"

"Yeah, we good brah." The two said together.

"Bet. We gone." Keem turned his music up some and pulled away from the curb, heading down P Street.

"Give me my money, fool." Crow said to his right-hand man.

Lil' One pilled off five blues and handed them over. "I wonder what the fuck he got us watchin' this nigga fo'?"

"I'on know. And I really don't give a fuck." Crow verbalized. "All I know is I'ma make this shit as easy as possible. Shid... five hundred a day. Just to sit on my ass. You can't beat that shit. My mama barely makin' that to bust her ass all week."

"No bullshit," Lil' One agreed. "That must be the nigga trap he keep runnin' in and out of." He assumed.

BM entered the backdoor of the apartment. The kitchen was his set up. The fentanyl he moved was so like that, it made it hard for him to find time to bag it all up. Every time a play would hit his phone, he'd have to hit the kitchen and make up whatever the request was. All he knew was that he'd be damned if he was dipping into his sack to eyeball even a tenth of a gram. He needed every dollar any which way that it came.

Focused as ever, BM felt good on the grind. So much so, that he could have sworn he'd found his third love. All was well. Yet, it felt as if there was something that just wasn't right. Each time before, he stepped back out the backdoor, BM made sure to take a peek out the window. He had noticed the two black cars parked on P Street. He'd never seen those cars around there before. At least, not parked on that street. He was smart enough to know that the cars didn't belong to a resident in one of the buildings that it was parked in front of. Looking out the window this time, he knew something wasn't right. Now, instead of two cars, there was only one. He hoped that for the occupants of the car that they were just visitors of the neighbors.

"BM!" A voice from behind him startled him out of spying on his unknown spies. He turned around and faced the person calling for his attention. "You okay?" A woman asked once she saw the sight of slight worry on his face. She was Tisha. His very first love. The exact same one he almost got his head blown off for. She was also, technically, the same reason BM's heart had turned so ill towards his one and only best friend. It'll be plenty of time to catch up on the happening on the two of them though. Because right now BM was in the middle of his all-time hustle.

"Yeah, everything Gucci." He stared at her as if she was the one acting weird. "Why you asked that?"

"I'on know. You're just actin' weird as a bitch. You movin' all sloppy, runnin' in and out and shit. Got people waitin' for you on the porch." Tisha pointed to the back door that was wide open. "You know me and my son still gotta live here, right? Or do you even give a fuck?" Notice how she said, 'my son' and not ours? Yeah, later on.

"The screen door locked, Tisha. I got dis. Carry yo ass back upstairs."

"Ight. I'm just makin' sure yo ass stayin' on point. That's it, that's all." She was already turned around, making her way up to the staircase.

BM took another peek out the window before he stepped back out the door. He thought the coast was clear, all besides that one suspicious car that he planned to check on later on. He couldn't have been further from the truth though.

Two blocks away, further out of BM's sight, was an all-black Crown Victoria. In the vehicle, were two people more experienced and equipped for a stake out. "Looks like he's selling drugs out of his girlfriend's house," Winchester said as he watched through a pair of binoculars.

"I swear," Calvez said as he slurped up a mouth full of ramen noodles out of the cup. "I don't know who's dumber? The men out here, or the women who allow them to use them."

"It's like he doesn't even give a fuck. I mean, it's clearly obvious what he's doing. Hope he doesn't think he's fooling anyone."

"What about the people in that car?" Calvez asked about the car that Lil' One and Crow sat in. "Did anyone get out of the car yet?"

"Nope. It's still sitting." Winchester replied. They were there the whole time the two cars had pulled up on P Street. Their antennas went up when they noticed the leading car pulling off, leaving the other behind. The real eye opener was no one got out of either car.

"I wonder what the fuck they're doing, just sitting there? Could just be some kids trying to figure out what their next moves are." Calvez concluded.

"What if they're watching the Macsby kid?" Winchester asked a question he thought was so bright that it made him lower the binoculars from his eyes.

"What you mean?" Calvez asked as if he was incompetent. "Like they're watching Macsby the way we are?" He searched for a better understanding of the questioned.

"Yeah, exactly." Winchester said, growing a little excited. "Maybe an enemy or something." Now they both were brainstorming.

"Could be right." Calvez got on board with the hypothesis. "Maybe, it's the shooter that targeted Foster. And now, he's back to finishing off the business with Macsby, thinking that Foster is already dead."

"That sounds about right." Detective Winchester almost agreed. "The only thing about that is, why haven't they made their move yet?"

"Good question, partner."

"I mean, they did have plenty of chances to off the kid by now." Winchester continued. "What's the hold up?"

"Maybe they see a two for one deal." Calvez assumed. Thinking as if he was the predator lurking for a kill himself.

"What do you mean?"

"Maybe they initially showed up for the kill. However, in the middle of waiting for the perfect timing, they noticed that the kid was bringing in some extra dollars. So, they—"

"Waited for the kid to sellout all the drugs. That way they could rob him right before the murder." Winchester finished off his partner's sentence once he caught on to the scenario.

"Exactly!" Detective Calvez proudly said, happy that his partner's chemistry was matching his frequency. "Sit back, partner. Looks like we're in for the long haul. And if were anywhere close to what we're thinking, we may even have a two-for-one deal for ourselves."

"Sounds like a plan to me."

LESSON 1.9
Check The Trap

On the corner of Lynnhaven Avenue and Lumkin Avenue, Keem pulled and parked the car. He had long ago dropped Shy off and left him with the rental car. Keem never took Shy along with him when he went on his business runs. As Keem stepped out of his Range Rover, his chain swung right and slight back left. The VVS diamonds sparkled at the touch of sunlight. The OGS abbreviation that hung from the chain was the biggest out of all the rest. The three letters stood for 'Organized Gang Shit'. That was the gang, and Keem was the honcho.

The house looked normal. Bleeding in with the others on the block. Habitable, but could use a lot of maintenance. You know, the regular poverty type shit. However, the one thing that was very up to date was the security. Before he could even approach the front door, whoever watched the cameras could already see him coming. The door unlocked at the perfect time, and Keem entered his headquarters.

"Hey, Keem." He was greeted as soon as he closed the door behind himself. The greeting woman wore laced drawers with a matching laced bra. The color was rose. She carried a clipboard in hand. With it, she kept the count of everything coming and everything going out. From all the drugs to all the money, down to the last grain and every single penny.

"Sup, Mia?" Keem replied. "What's the count? Everything good with the business?"

As Keem asked the question, Mia walked behind him with a look of worry spread across her face. The windows in the living room were covered with wooden boards. Purposely. Those same boards could be retracked, if need be, with the push of a button.

Keem headed towards the kitchen as he awaited a reply from Mia. Once he realized that the answer was prolonged, he stopped in his tracks. With a stern look upon his face, Keem turned around to face Mia. Just by the expression on her face, he could tell that something wasn't right.

"The count is off," Mia said reluctantly. With a little fear of Keem's response.

Mia basically had two main counts to keep up with. The incoming count was the total amount of all the money that came in on a daily, weekly, monthly, quarterly, and annual basis. Being that Keem had multiple shops set up throughout the city, and in a few cases, even beyond, Mia had to keep count of who brought in what from where. The other count was the outgoing count of the drugs that were distributed to the branches of crews that Keem rooted. The only count that Keem kept for himself was the amount of drugs he got from his plug Mac.

"Did you count again?" Keem tried his best to remain calm. As good as he succeeded, one of the main things he hated was for his money to be fucked up. Especially if it was due to somebody else fucking it up. Still though, he wanted to make sure that she hadn't made the mistake herself before he paid the consequences to someone else.

"I counted three times." Mia was honest. Thus far, she had never made a mistake with the count. She was precisely accurate and slightly trusted. And although that slight amount of trust was light, it was heavy to be trusted by at all. Yet alone, slightly trusted. "But I can count again if you need me to make sure."

CRIME PAYS | SELF MADE TAY

"Naw, you good." Keem paused his request. "You did yo job. Thank you." He turned around and continued to walk towards the kitchen. "Where is the shortage comin' from?" He questioned Mia as his eyes roamed the happenings of his operation. In the kitchen were two tables. They each were placed far apart on opposite sides of the kitchen. An island sat directly in the middle. One table was used for breaking down bricks of heroin. The one on the opposite side was used for the marijuana while the island being closer to the stove was used for the breaking down and or transformation of the cocaine into crack. Depending on whatever the orders were for the workload.

"It's Mo from First Avenue." Mia hated that she had to be the one to break the news, but she got paid plenty of money to do so. Besides, if not sent right in this situation, the messenger would get killed. "He said that—"

"I'on wanna hear what that nigga said." Keem put a hand up saving Mia a waist of breath. "If it ain't the money talking, it ain't none to talk about."

Mia said nothing in response. Keem kept his composure on the surface. There was no need for him to make no one else pay for the failure of another man. Deep down inside though, he was boiling. Not only was this Mo's second time being late short this month, but this was the fourth time in the last quarter.

For the sake of generosity and understanding, Keem usually gave his people the *three strikes and you're out* pitch. Going against his better judgement, he gave Mo an inch too many. Now, he regretted it. He really didn't care about how short the money was. He had extras put aside just for that purpose. He understood how the game went at times. It had its highs and lows. It just came with the hustle. With Mo though, it was a sign of disrespect. Keem felt as if he was being taken advantage of.

Mo thought he could get away with more than the others could. He felt privileged. As if he could fuck up time after time and wouldn't have to deal with the consequences. He became accustomed to Keem giving him the hustler's motivation speech. Little did he know though, Keem was tired of talking. Mo saw him and Keem as brothers. He looked at Keem like family because Keem had a son with Mo's sister. Keem saw Mo as a liability. Someone who was always in the fucking way. Although Mo was older than Keem, he still put him on his feet in hopes that he would run up a bag. Mo's problem was that he thought he was already on Keem's level just because of association.

Keem scrolled through the contacts of his phone until he spotted Simon's name. Clicking on the contact, he dialed the number.

"Aye Simon," Keem said over the phone. "Code Red. 3 AM." Was all Keem stated before quickly ending the call. The throw-off to the code was really as basic as it could get. Everything was said in flip flop. Simon was really a big fish. A shark as a matter of fact. The code red was really the code blue. The color blue represented ice. When that code was called, it was time to freeze a nigga. The three, was really nine. Because that was the opposite number on the standard clock. And the AM was PM. Nine o'clock tonight, it was going down.

LESSON 1.10
Tables Will Turn

Later on, that day, E was processed out of the hospital and right into to the Richmond City Jail. The procedure took so long that it was starting to hit nightfall by the time he made it to the tier in general population.

He was tired after losing two peers due to death by the hands of gun violence. They came empty handed on a robbery and him getting shot and slimed out by his best friend and then watching him escape through the backdoor. He ended up leaving surgery with a fractured rib. Then, being charged and locked up for possession of crack-cocaine with the intent to distribute. Along with the possession of a firearm with the possession of a scheduled one substance and being told that he was denied bond. With the news that he was facing a mandatory minimum of seven years at the least, E thought that his coming into the new year couldn't get any worse. *How could it,* he wondered. There was no way possible. At least, that's what he thought.

On the fifth floor of the jail, E had to enter through two different doors to land on the 5 -E tier. The first thing he did was, lean his folded mat along with sheets and blanket up against the wall on the floor. He scanned the tier for any familiar faces. Looking for either allies or enemies. He recognized a few. But none of them were on the ally side. "Back already, huh Foster?" The CO asked kind of disappointed but not too much surprised. And definitely not tripping, seeing that it was job security for him. "You just left, what, right before Halloween, right?"

" What's up Jones?" E spoke to the male CO, who was only older than him by maybe a couple years. "Yeah. It was some like that." Talking to the CO, E never took his eyes off his fellow inmates. In return, they all had their eyes turned right back towards him. Some scared, stealing stares. A few mugged hatefully. Most watched just to be nosey while the rest looked on just to be aware. "What cell they got me going too?" He asked.

"Cell 17" The CO Jones simply replied.

"Who in there?"

"An old head. Pretty laid back. Cool. You good with that?" Jones was new to the job. A cool CO. It was almost two years ago when E remembered breaking Jones in as a CO. Jones was quieter back then. A little timid. Now a days, he has opened up more. Talked a lot more shit. But still kept his laid-back demeanor. Jones's first impression of E was that he was one of the wildest young niggas in the jail. Running phones and extorting people for them, in and out of fights and back and forth to the hole. What made matters even worst was that E and BM had been on the tier together with a tier full of Mosby niggas. This time, from the looks of it so far, the tables had turned.

"Yeah, I'm good." E sounded a little unsure.

"You sure?" Jones searched for clarification.

"Yeah, pop my cell," E said. Jones pushed a button on the panel on the computer screen and unlocked cell 17. The cell was located all the way in the back of the triangle shaped tier. E grabbed his mat and other belongings and traveled towards his destination. To him, it seemed as if the walk took forever. Not only was his rib causing extreme pain with every step that he took but the stares felt as if they were drilling a hole right through his skull.

"Yeah. That's the nigga, E." He could hear the whispers of the chatter on the tier. "That bitch ass nigga shot my cousin," someone mumbled. Knowing exactly who it was, E smiled on the inside. "I'm surprised dude ain't trying to check off this bitch." He looked around as he moved through, trying to match the faces with the many voices he was hearing. "That nigga better not say a word while he on this tier." The voices were starting to grow so rapidly that it became hard for him to distinguish them. It was almost as if he was reading minds. He couldn't actually see anyone talking but could hear the voices. "Hope that nigga don't think he 'bout to get on one of them phones." It damn near drove him crazy in the short period of time. "Yeah. That nigga from Mosby. That's BM right hand."

The thing that was worse than the continuation of the voices, was the energy that topped it times two. Just off the vibrations in the air, E could definitely feel that it was going to go down. The thing he didn't know though, was exactly when. He made it to his cell safely, walked in, and turned around to make sure no one tried to follow him inside. He threw his belongings on the top bunk and placed his back to the wall in the back of the cell. He waited for a moment as he gathered his thoughts.

"These bitch ass niggas," he said to himself out loud. "Twelve gotta be setting a nigga up. Puttin me on a tier with all these ma'fuckin' opps. They know what the fuck be goin' on." The unit he had landed on was filled with mostly Jackson Ward and Creighton niggas. They both were arch rivalries of Mosby Court. The only good thing that E may have going for himself was that, at the time, Jackson Ward and Creighton were smack dead in the middle of a beef of their own. Still though, either way it went, E was outnumbered regardless. One thing he was most definitely sure of was that checking off the tier was not even an option. He'd much rather die. Going out fighting for his life literally than to be a running coward.

"Foster! Come on, let's go!" E could hear Jones rushing him out of the cell. "I gotta go. I need you to close that door back." Down the jail the CO's did their best at keeping the cell doors locked. Every now and then they would do a cell break, allowing the inmates to go in and grab a few items. Or stay in until the next cell breaks. Otherwise, the doors stayed locked. Especially, when there was no CO present on the tier. It keeps the trouble down a lot more that way.

E walked to the door and stepped just outside the cell. "Aight," he yelled up to the CO that was still all the way at the front of the tier. "Go head!" He tried to convince Jones. "I'm trying to make my bed and shit up." He lied trying to buy himself some time. "Plus, I gotta take a shit." That part was the truth.

"Come on Foster, you know I can't leave the unit with the cell door open." E ignored the CO and walked back into the cell still leaving the door open. Jones was growing frustrated. He figured he'd get in one more round before he exited the tier. E fumbled with his sheets and mattress as if he had really planned to make it up. Truthfully, he had no idea what the hell he was about to do. A part of him wanted to get it over with and go out into the day room, popping the first opp he came in contact with. With the CO on the tier though, that would be too close to tipping. He couldn't see himself coming anywhere close to breaking lesson 1.6.

The other part wanted him to wait until it came to him. Maybe them niggas were too afraid to even lay a hand on him. Maybe they were smart and didn't want to deal with the backlash on the streets that came with fucking with a nigga like E. But playing the waiting game kind of fucked with his anxiety a little too much. It pushed his nerve to their breaking point. Plus, he asked himself *'what would he do if the shoe was on the other foot?'* What if he was sitting at other end of the table? Exactly. He'd take the opportunity to step on his opposition like walking over a crowd of ants, swallowing them whole like a shark would do a school of fish.

"Aye Foster." E turned towards the cell door to catch CO Jones standing in the doorway. "You sure you good? I'on want none to happen on my watch. I'm just tryna get my check and carry my ass. You already know how I roll."

"Yeah, I know you ain't on shit Jones. I was just sayin' I'ma need a few extra minutes to get myself together. I ain't tryna hold you though. You good, I'll close the door when I'm done."

"You know damn well I can't do that, Foster."

"You can do whatever the fuck you wanna do. Besides, what can you do 'bout some you don't know none 'bout." For a few seconds, they both stared each other down. Saying nothing while saying a lot at the same exact time.

"Aight, well look. Make my job easier and at least walk out the cell with me and act like you closin' the door. That way, it'll look good on camera." E thought for a second. He only replied by making his way towards the door. "Look like you 'bout to do something crazy. I would tell you not to but I know it ain't no stoppin' you when you got yo' mind made up." Jones walked away from the door and E exited the cell faking as if he closed the cell. No less than three minutes later, Jones was walking off the tier without even bothering to look back.

As soon as the second door going off the tier had slid closed and Jones had headed down the hallway, walking out of sight, niggas were making their way towards to E. Everybody stopped everything they were doing and focused all their attention towards the back of the tier. Well, everybody except the niggas that were on the phone. All except one continued their conversations. They spoke in soft whispering tones about how it was about to go down on the unit. The one out of four that hung up their phone calls were one of the main ones that wanted to see E's blood leaking from his mouth.

E quickly opened the door to his cell. Posted in a stance of defense, he stood in the doorway and bravely awaited the attack that was inevitable.

Being that he was the closest enemy to E, the one that had just hung up the phone, had got to him first. He was about two and a half inches taller than E, so mathematically, he had the reach on him as well. E's pivot foot was glued to the ground as if it was a sheet of paper. He swung the other foot a few degrees to the back. The swing came forcefully and from a distance. E eyed it, timing it with precision. He ducked. The blow missed him by half of second. With all the strength he could muster, Keem countered with a quick uppercut with his right. It contacted aggressively underneath the chin. The blow was unexpected and effective. Just wasn't quite enough to put the opponent out of commission.

The attacker returned with a blind jab with his left. It caught E directly under his right eye. E's left hook was already on the way. It contacted the jaw of his target but it caused E more pain than he was able to dish out. He almost doubled over towards his left from the sharp excruciating pain that he felt in his rib. Noticing the slight hesitation in E's movement, the fighter detected that something wasn't right. He took another punch to the face from E in order to counter with a right hook to E's side. Figuring he had no other option; he took a few steps backwards into the cell.

By now, the whole tier was attentive on the fight. Even the ones who tried their best to act as if they weren't. "Rush that nigga Pound!" Another person ordered standing right outside the door. "Fuck you waitin' on?" The motivation along with seeing E back away from the fight, kind of boasted Pound's ego a little too high. Throwing hands back up, he took small steps towards E and went in swinging madly wild.

With the proper footwork, E could spare a good five to six inches between his back and the wall. He took two steps backwards. Counted two swings from his opposition that only blew wind. Then, he took one step up and landed a powerful blow squarely in the middle of his face. Immediately, the first sight of blood was drawn.

Pound couldn't feel it at first. But soon did. The pain was so alarming that he placed his hands up to it and was pissed when he brought it back down. The palm of his hand was covered in his own blood. Pound grew enraged like a bull that saw red.

"You bitch!" Pound screamed angrily rushing E for a third time. E ducked the blows again coming up to the right side. He landed a right the jaw. Then, made it a two-piece combo when he added a quick jab the nose.

Pound doubled over. He covered his head in an attempt to protect his nose. With the bottom of his foot, E sent a crushing kick to the top of Pound's head. The kick caused Pound to fall backwards, landing on his ass like a baby taking his first steps.

"The fuck out my cell pussy," E barked. He only spared Pound the extra beat down out of pure intelligence. He knew that someone who was pissed off at what had just happened to his homeboy would try their hands. Win, lose, or draw them Jackson Ward boys never went out without a fight. E knew he had to save his energy because another one was coming.

Someone had ran into the cell, cupping Pound underneath his armpits. The person dragged him out backwards to safety. As soon as Pound was clear, another individual immediately rushed the cell. He was a little more skilled than Pound. Instead of going with the quickness, he used his wits. Hands up, toe to toe, they squared up. They both waited for the first swing. Just from watching the last fight, the second fighter realized that E was good at ducking and dodging blows. Even better, he was great at counteracting. He was curious to see what it would come with on the offensive side.

"Let's go pussy." The second fighter taunted, trying to piss E off and force him into making an irrational decision. It didn't work.

E was thinking. He knew the fighter across from him well enough. Good enough to know that his chest was full of heart. The streets called him Taz caused he spun like the Tasmanian Devil from Looney Toon. Once before, in a shootout, E and Taz had stood toe to toe throwing bullet after bullet at their targets, which was each other.

Now, here they stood still looking to do harm. But instead of using bullets, they would use their body parts. Still though, E sensed that Taz had some type of second thought about attacking him. He used that to his advantage.

E threw a pump fake with the right bucking at Taz. It caused him to throw up a block with his left arm. Immediately switching it up, E doubled back with a quick jab with the left. From there the fight commenced. Taz was pissed that he had been outsmart. Saying fuck it, Taz threw jab after jab landing three out of five to E's face. Doing the same, E returned jabs of his own. They went blow for blow. Pound for Pound. The punches were so hard that they sounded off throughout the cell. From the sideline, a few ohhs and awws could be heard, along with a few damns. Damn near, if not everyone, was against E, making him the underdog. But even a few realists had to admit that this was one of the best fights they've seen in a while. E was a soldier with the heart of a lion. But still though, with a fractured rib and bullet wounds fresh in his body, E was at a disadvantage. The adrenaline took his mind off the pain for a few minutes. But soon it was hard to ignore. E grabbed Taz around the neck with his right arm trying to lock up with him. He threw a few left hooks landing all of them to Taz's jaw. Taz threw two jabs to the left side of E's body.

"Agghhh…" E screamed out so painfully loud that it even scared Taz. E cocked his head back and threw it forward, landing a headbutt to Taz's forehead. The contact dazed Taz for a few seconds. If it wasn't for the lock that E had on him, it would have caused Taz to stumble or possibly fall even.

The panic made Taz shake back quickly. He grew nervous as he felt a drip of blood in his eye. He wrapped both of his arms around E, lifted him up, and took him for a ride slamming him to the floor. The thud shook the floor a little. As soon as the two hit the ground, a handful of niggas rushed the cell. Each and every last one of them immediately put hands and feet on E's body. All E could do was ball up on the ground. Wisely, he laid on his left side protecting his bruised rib from the attack.

"Twelve, twelve, twelve!" The tier yelled out. Giving a heads up that the CO was on the way back on the tier. Everyone that was in the cell quickly snuck out as if they were never there. Taz was the last one to exit the cell. Before he did, he looked down at E and spat on him. "That's for my cousin. Pussy bitch," Taz said before leaving E laying on the floor by his lonesome. So many fucked up thoughts went through E's mind that it depressed him. For the second time, within the last 24 hours, he was left lying on the floor alone, injured, and fighting to live. He was more than relieved when the abuser crawled up off of him.

"Get up right fast young blood." E heard a voice say to him as a man walked into the cell. The next sound he heard was the mattress being slid off the top bunk. "At least make it look like you sleep," he suggested. "Unless you want the CO to find you like this." E thought but didn't respond. Instead, he slowly peeled himself off the floor. "I'ma throw the sheets over yo' mat and lay it on the floor, so you can look like you in here sleep." It was E's cellie. Crazy part was that he was from Jackson Ward himself. After living over half a century, the old head knew better than to intervene with the laws of karma. "Go head and lay it down for the night youngin. I'ma clean this blood up off this floor and lock this cell so you can get some rest." The old head did as he promised and left E to recuperate.

LESSON 1.11
Never Show Weakness

Five minutes before nine o'clock PM, Keem pulled up to 1st Avenue around Northside Richmond. It was the Highland Park area of the city. He stepped out of the car and walked a few cars up, getting into the black Yukon Denali. No words were spoken. The car pulled off and stopped only a few blocks up the same street.

"Yeah, we outside," Simon said over the phone sitting in the passenger seat of the SUV. "Nigga bring yo' ass outside! You know how we do business. Shit ain't none new. Simon was like a two for one hire for Keem. He was the number one collector of bodies as well as currency. So, whenever he was sent to collect, he was hardly ever, if ever at all, played with. "Niggas always tryna try a nigga," Simon said after hanging up the phone.

They sat outside of Keem's baby's mother house. Mo thought that they were there to make a collection transaction but boy was he ever wrong. On top of that, he had absolutely no idea that Keem was present as well. "Don't trip, Simon. We 'bout to get rid of this clumsy ass nigga once and for all. Nigga won't have to trip again," Keem announced.

Mo came swagging out his sister's front door with his cell phone to his ear. Three of his ten fingers had nice size diamond fluttered rings on them. A gold Rolex was wrapped around his left wrist. The face of the Rolex was bust down with VVS diamonds. His members only, OGS chain swung around his neck. And both the top and the bottom of his teeth were like a dance floor for diamonds. "That's why the nigga can't make the payments," Simon commented with a disappointing sigh. "Nigga out here living like a fuckin' rapper or somethin'. Look like he 'bout to go to a fuckin' video shoot or somethin'."

"Fool don't even know he 'bout to go straight to his grave." The driver chuckled lightly.

"I hope his bitch ass got insurance," Keem stated. He was pissed at the sight of MO. One thing Keem hated was to be taken advantage of. "Because if it's gone be up to me, the nigga gone have the cheapest funeral that money can buy. Get his ass buried in aluminum foil fuckin' with me." Both the driver and Simon let out historical laughs. "Aye Si, open the door for that bitch ass nigga."

"Gotcha boss." Simon climbed his 6-foot 5-inch frame from out of the front passenger seat and grabbed the handle of the back door on his side of the car.

"What the fuck is this?" Mo asked with sarcastic humor. His loud voice could be heard inside the SUV as he drew closer towards it. "Niggas opening doors and shit now? About time you notice a real boss when you see one my nigga." Simon opened the door slowly with an ingenuine smile spread across his face. "Damn nigga, hurry the fuck up my nigga! I got my bitch waiting on—" MO words were stopped like vehicles at a red light. "Keem, what's up brah?" MO changed up. The look on Keem's face said it all. "What the hell you " Mo tried to take a step backwards and bumped right into Simon.

"Get yo' bitch ass in there!" Simon pushed MO back forward, forcing him into the backseat of the Denali. "We goin' for a ride. Boss!" Simon said sarcastically, reminding MO of the boss that he thought he was.

" What's up Keem?" Mo immediately started to sweat beads. Simon climbed into the backseat and closed the door behind him. Sitting in between the two of those men had Mo scared as hell. So much so, that he didn't even realize that he had dropped the phone in his lap without hanging it up.

Keem ignored the greeting. Leaving the car so silent that the woman could be heard from the other end of the phone. "Hello? Hello? Mo!" Keem looked over at Simon and gestured down towards the phone. Mo caught the gesture and picked up the phone out of his lap attempting to place it to his ear. Before he could even do so, Simon snatched out of his hand. Next, Simon pulled a glove out his pants pocket. With the job that he worked, they came in handy every now and then. He used his shirt to wipe down the phone, placed the glove on his hand, and used the gloved hand to smash the phone on the concrete. "Let's go!" Simon indicated to his driver to pull off as he rolled the window back up.

"Come on man," Mo was already beginning to pledge his plea. "I told Mia I was gone get the money."

"You think this shit is about money, Mo?" Keem asked, cutting off Mo's cry. "You can't really think that this shit is 'bout money, my nigga."

"Shid... it can't be none else my nigga 'cause I—"

"You know what a boss is Mo?" Keem questioned. The inquiry left Mo silent, looking stupid. "A boss is one that make sures his people eat. Not take food out there mouths. Are you the one that make sure this team eat?" Mo remained silent. So, Keem answered the question for him. "No. You're not. As a matter of fact, nigga yo' ass is taking food away from the team's table."

"Mane, listen brah. I'll pay that shit back double. Shid... triple, if I have too." Mo was trying to throw money at Keem. Not knowing that it was only pissing him off even more.

"Naw! You listen ma'fucka!" Keem raised his voice. For a man that allowed his actions to speak for him, Keem hated to have to raise his voice. "You had yo' chance to talk. Actually, one too many for this line of business. You've even had a chance to shut up and let yo' money talk for you. Now it's time to shut up and listen.

"See, you fucked up when you thought it was all about the money. Don't let me get it fucked up because money plays a major role. But sometimes, a nigga can have all the money in the world. Shit won't mean shit without a man havin' principles. The game gone school him. A man with money that has no love will be hated. I've seen money destroy the weakest ma'fucka because all they did was flex. A boss doesn't get caught up in all that. He has balance. He knows when to be a savage and when to be a gentleman. A boss doesn't measure himself up to another man. He runs his own race at his own pace. He doesn't allow the pressure of fame to cause him to become disloyal. And he definitely won't bite the hand that feeds him.

"You not a fuckin' boss. My nigga you a leech. You out this bitch faking like you got yo' paper right. Like you fuckin' hustla of the year or somethin'. Meanwhile, you living under yo' lil sista roof and don't help her pay not one bill. How dare you claim to be a boss? Tryna shit on me. Out here carrying the team. What you ain't know nigga? You gotta carry yo' own weight."

For Mo, it felt like a very long ride to nowhere but just down the street. Before Keem could even realize it, they were already at their destination. The driver of the SUV parked at a dead-end road and hit the lights. From the mountain they were on, Keem looked over the Over-by Sheppard elementary school. He didn't feel bad at all for what he was about to do. As a matter of fact, he felt as if Mo did it to himself. Either way he looked at it though, it had to be done. There was a snake in the grass. So, it had to be cut, both the snake and the grass. Who knew what other types of disloyal traits that Mo may have in him? His next trick may have been to rob Keem. Or maybe even kill him. How was Keem to know if Mo would've took a shot at the throne? Even worst, what if Mo's flashiness would have gotten him in trouble with the law and he traded Keem in for his own freedom, giving the police all types of information that brought the whole team down? One thing Keem would and could not do was sit back and wait for those questions to be answered.

"Take him out," Keem ordered Simon. Following the plan, Simon opened the door and yanked out Mo's small body frame with one hand. He placed a pistol to the back of Mo's head and demanded him to move.

"Try some stupid shit if you want. I'ma bust yo' dumb ass," Simon promised.

"Turn the truck around," Keem ordered. The driver did just that. When the car stopped again after making a U-turn, now parked in the other direction, Keem stepped out and calmly made his way into the darken woods. The location was call 'The White Mountains' by the Highland Park community. The ground of the wooded mountain was always covered with this white type fungus. All season round it remained the same.

Going deep enough in the woods, Keem came up on Simon and Mo awaiting his approach. "Come on Keem, man please, don't do this my nigga." Mo begged as tears started to flow down his cheeks. The begging didn't faze Keem, not one bit. He didn't have a word to utter. In fact, Keem never wanted to say anything to Mo at all from the jump. The words he spoke earlier were really a message to the driver and Simon. A reminder on how important it was to remember who the boss was. He could have easily had Mo killed for next to nothing. But being that Keem brought him into the game, it was right that he took him out as well. Keem snatched Mo's OGS chain from around his next without even uttering a word.

Keem removed the pistol from his waist band, upping it immediately to Mo's eye level.

Bow!

The shot rung throughout the darkness of the woods. Mo's body fell instantly in the very same spot he had just stood. Keem gave Simon a look. Simon knew exactly what it meant. He aimed the gun at Mo's already dead body and placed two more bullets into his corpse. Bocca! Bocca! Keem was already halfway back to the SUV with Simon right on his trail.

Keem was driven back to his car. Before he got into his vehicle, he left the gun with Simon. Climbing behind the wheel, Keem drove two minutes down the street and parked in front of his babies mother's house. He went in, fucked her brains out, and stayed there for the rest of the night. Alibi certified. Keem was ahead of the game as always. And that's what made him the mastermind of the group. The boss. Real honcho.

LESSON 1.12

Four Horsemen

In downtown Richmond, the government had courts that handled criminal and other justice affairs. On the next block over was city hall, which handled business, school board, and all types of other civil matters. There even were the mayors' and governors' mansion not too far from the very project's they subtly dictated.

Right under all of their noses were the governors' of the streets. There was a master mind group that called themselves the Four Horsemen of the city of Richmond. They were the corner stones that connected the capstone together. They were so discreet that a good eighty-five percent of the city never even knew they existed. Some people even knew one of the four Horsemen. But never knowing that he was a part of a square such as the Four Horsemen. Like, Mac for example. He was well known in the city of Richmond. But yet, barely known at all. He represented the East End section of the city's square.

The other three members also represented a large section of the square of the city. There was Brick from the Jackson Ward area. He controlled most of the downtown area along with the whole Northside Richmond. Dawg from West End called the shots for the West End of the city. Then Black, well of course, his dominion was the Southside of Richmond, which was south of the James River.

Once a week, the men got together for a meeting that no one could attend except for them. To the rest of the city the meeting never exists. You could have told someone about it, and they would have never believed you. The four Horsemen created a pyramid scheme. Everyone that had their hands in the dirt was being watched and accounted for in some type of way.

"Morning gentlemen," Mac greeted as he entered the hotel suite. The location was Downtown at the Jefferson Hotel. The place was antique, and full of luxury riches. Each men had a total of four meeting spots. Every week they changed up places to meet accordingly. Today was a day to meet up at one of Brick's meeting places and the Jefferson Hotel was one of his favorites. In fact, it was one of all four of their favorites.

"Welcome Mac," Brick greeted before taking a puff on one of the most expensive cigars that money could buy. He was tailored in an all-gray suit that shinned a little silver. With dark blue tie, short, and cuff links he resembled a cloud of ether.

"Looks like someone decided to take it back to the nineties," Mac said more in a statement rather than a joke. "I like. It speaks volumes to yo' class." Mac sported a red blazer with rose gold accessories. His red bottom Louie Vuitton dress shoes topped it off perfectly, like a cherry on top of a Sundae ice cream.

"Looks like you came with a lil' competition this week," Brick joked lightly with Mac.

"Are you niggas models or mobstas? Dawg asked taking a seat one of the four throne's of The Four Horsemen at the far end of the table.

"Oh, but looks who's talking?" Mac quickly responded while admiring Dawg's peaches and cream three-piece suit. "Every week you show up, you be on yo' pretty boy shit."

92

"Aye," Dawg replied as he popped both sides of his collar on his peach jacket. In order to play the part, you have to look it. Right?"

"And you do them both well, my friend," Mac complemented. "Appreciate that, Mac."

"Black, what's up what's up?" Mac greeted. "You going to hit a lick after the meeting, or now?" Black was covered in all black everything. The black on black was fresh and crisp. Fitting Black's physic to a tighten tee. "Bad enough you already black as hell." Mac snuck in a little but truthful joke. His objective was to get Black to lighten up a little. "What's up what's up? You good?" He sensed that something just wasn't right with his partner in crime.

"Them lil' mafuckas out Hillside" Black stated with a little hint of stress in his tone. "Lil' niggas been shootin' shit up for last seven days straight now. Four fuckin' bodies dropped in one fuckin' week with about nine. And that's in Hillside alone."

Mac took a seat on his throne along with the other kings at the table. "Yeah, shit ain't been looking too good in the East end either. Especially in Mosby. My own fuckin' hood, which is what pisses mean off the most. What makes the matter even worst, is that it's my own fuckin' son that's the main one causin' me the headache."

BM always been a problem in these streets," Brick reminded.

"Yeah, but I think has finally lost his fuckin' mind. He even tried to kill his own best friend, E."

"Or maybe he found his mind. You still don't think he's ready?" Dawg asked.

"I'on think that fool gone ever be ready," Mac confessed. "He's so pissed at me and his mother, he done took it out on the whole damn world."

"You never know," said Dawg. "Kid could be at his breakin' point."

"Time will tell," Mac brushed off any hopes of BM elevation. "Black, you know I can get Keem on that Hillside situation, right? Them lil' niggas love him out there. Be hangin' on to his every word." Mac opted to change the subject.

"Yeah, I know," Black assured. "But I'd much rather let the rug rats get the shit out there system. In due time, the street will clear up. Then, the real hustlas will be able to pop back out without havin' to worry 'bout gettin' shot by a stray or locked up for mistaken identity. Just don't understand why these young niggas don't want any real fuckin' money." Black shook his head while rubbing a finger up against his temple.

"Da lil' niggas round the Ward got there hustle up," Brick spoke up for his side of the town. "They just keep fuckin' it up tryna keep up with rappers image. I mean, I'on really have a problem with it as long as my count ain't fucked up." I do wish they would take it to the next level though. It's 'bout that time for them. The Northside numbers are up double than usual. Mostly due to the Boulevard and North Ave, Washington Park, and Delmont and St. Lukes area. But they dropping round Highland Park. A few dick heads done got together and decided to rob all the spots."

"You figured out who the team was yet?" Dawg question.

"Yeah," Brick replied. "Come to find out the brains of the operation is a woman. She gets close to all the head niggas of the spots and take the drops back to her team."

"Smart as hell if you ask me," Mac commented. "Not original, but smart by hitting some new dogs with an old trick. So, what's the plan to stop 'em?"

"We got a temporary spot we 'bout to set up on Chestnut. Take all the attention down that way. Draw them into a hole and set the trap. they'll be dead in a week or so." Brick convinced his comrades.

"Let us know if you need some help with that," Mac offered.

"Already," replied Brick. "So, let's get to the big business of the week. What's the word on closin' them deals with the banks?"

"They still not budging on the offer.' Dawg reported the bad news. There were a small branch of banks that were originated in Richmond. There were only three in total, and the four horsemen wanted them all.

"I say we rob them ma'fuckas," Brick suggested. "Let 'em know that they would need a lil more protection other than them security guards and cameras. Show 'em exactly how much they actually need us. I bet then they'll allow us to buy in."

"Sounds like a plan if you ask me," Mac voted with agreement.

"Bet, I'll get lady on it within the next three days. Once she gets hired, we can work from the inside and start the plot," Dawg announced his agreement to the idea.

"What y'all think 'bout a drought?" Black asked completely out the blue.

"You mean like right now?" Mac questioned.

"Shidd... I ain't tripping," Dawg replied. "I could use a break."

"Yeah," Black responded to Mac's question. "Give 'em a lil extra and then next week, we pull the plug. Cut the fuckin water off." Black took a shot from his glass of champagne.

"Why now though?" Mac was curious. He was good on his numbers and a drought wouldn't hurt his count at all. Truthfully, it was Keem he was thinking about. He had been moving up so steadily and smoothly that a setback would place plenty of static in Keem's vision.

"Cuz, I bet if we starve the streets for a few, it'll make 'em hungry. Force 'em to eat." Black had the thought in mind for a few weeks now. He tried to hold back on the idea to see if the death toll and shootings would calm down, but they didn't. "Besides, it'll speed up this killin' spree these ma'fuckas been on. Since they want to make it killin' season, we'll let it be that."

Mac sat back and thought hard and long for a few seconds. The other three members allowed him the time to contemplate his thoughts. He leaned forward on his throne with his elbows rested on the arms of the chairs. "What's yo' vote on dis, Brick?

"I say we stack it up for a week or two and then go on vacation. Fuck it. Shit, the wife been beggin' for the Bahamas again anyway. I could kill two birds with one stone."

"Well, I guess a vacation it is then." Mack threw in the final agreement for his fellow Horsemen and himself to dry the city up. "But I think I may do my distribution a lil different this time," Mac alerted the table.

"Like how?" Brick wondered.

"Keem," Mac simply responded before raising his glass to take a sip. "Instead of hitting all my clientele off, I think I just want to lay it all on him. That way while we're gone, he won't have to miss a beat with his hustle.

"You don't think that's a bad idea?" Dawg wanted to know.

"Yeah, like you don't think that would be too much for the youngin?" Black added.

"Naw, I think the kid could really manage." Mac was fully confident in his speech. "Besides, it's only one way to find out, right?"

"So, you really believe in this kid, huh?" Dawg searched for conviction.

"Yep," Mac said without a hint of doubt. "More than any of them niggas."

"Okay. So, you believe that his hustle is strong." Brick basically repeated in search of confirmation. "But what about his mind? Do you think his ego could handle the next level?"

"To be honest, I think that the kid is so confident in himself that the insecure would mistake it for cockiness. Yet, he's so levelheaded. He's a humbled winner. I think it's his vision that keeps him grounded. He know how far he's came. But remains focused on how far he has to go. I really believe that he will have is shit together in the future." Mac paused to take an extra sip of the champagne that rested in the glass. As he sipped, he allowed the words he had just spoken to sink into the other master minds brain. As they did, Mac could see the thoughts change their facial expressions.

"Wow Mac," Dawg stated, "Thats heavy. I'm kinda excited to see exactly how he handles the load." Even though I advise you not to place all eggs in one basket. But on the other hand, I've learned the hard way to not to go against yo' judgement."

"Naw don't trip. If he fuck it up, which I doubt, I got the cleanup." Mac wanted to erase any worry that the team may have had. "And besides, the kid deserves the opportunity." Mac confessed. "I put him to the test, and he passed with flyin' colors."

"Yeah, I meant to ask you how that situation went," Brick said.

"Perfectly, as planned," Mac announced.

"You know what?" A bright light had glowed up in Brick's mind. "I got an even better idea. Since the niggas I'm fuckin wit can't seem to keep they puppies on a leash, how about I leave Keem with my load percentage as well? That is, if you think he can handle it."

"I'm sure he could." Mac confidently confided.

"Shidd. He might as well take mine too then," Brick offered. "Like I said, numbers were doubled on the Northside and in Highland Park getting robbed blind. So, I might as well let Keem get some flips in. Jus make sure he gets in touch with somebody around the Ward. I can't do the home team dirty. They been grindin' like never before."

"Say no more," Mac said. "I'll get the word to his ear," he promised.

"Even though I think this would be too much for the kid's plate and a bad idea, I don't see why I would hand anybody else work while the rest of the city is dry. No need to place everyone in competition with Keem. Especially, since his hands will be full. So, therefore, I'll give him mine as well."

"Trust me, my friend." Mac raised his glass once more. "Y'all will not be disappointed. This is to the vacation." The other three Horsemen raised their glasses and clang them up against each other's.

"To a vacation," they all said in union. They took shots and lit up cigars. Afterwards, they ate their weekly meals and small talked on other big plans. Worry free.

LESSON 1.13
Utilize Pawns

"Come on, Baby Mac," a fiend was in the middle of begging. "You know I'ma bring you yo' money back. And if not, then you know I'ma bring you some plays from round here."

"I told you don't call me that shit." BM practically ignored what the fiend lady was saying. "My name BM."

"Boy you know what I mean. Come on though. Stop bullshittin' me and come on so a bitch can get high."

"Naw you the one on bullshit. Wit that bullshit ass money."

The lady was trying to get twenty dollars' worth of Fentanyl with only four dollars in cash and some change. "Plus, yo' ass just left twenty minutes ago. Talking 'bout you tryna get high. Bitch you as high as a bitch right now." BM sat on the back of Tisha's porch. The same place he'd been at for the pass twenty-four hours or so. As of now, he was counting up the money that he had accumulated throughout the day. It was only earlier when he had ran into Pike. Just off the Fentanyl alone, BM had made his money back and was halfway towards a double up. Within the next hour, it would be approaching midnight soon. The first one of the new year. BM thought it would be smart to catch Pike on the re-up tonight. That way, he could be sure to have a fresh and full sake for the morning rush.

Stuffing the money in his pocket, BM looked up at the fiend. He was about to curse her ass out before sending her on her way. As he looked passed her, he thought of a win-win situation. That could work out in both of their favors. "Matter of fact," BM stated. "Give me that four dollars."

"Okay, that's what I'm talking about, my nigga."

Happily, she handed over the four dollars. Next, she tried to give BM the change.

"Naw, keep the change." He rejected the coins.

"Shidd… bet. I can get me some loosies wit this." She slid the change back in her pocket and waited to receive the drug.

"You gotta put in some work to replace the rest of that payment." BM broke the news to her. He had a mission for her. All day, he had thought about doing it himself. But, figured that it would be too risky. Because, if what he thought was true, then they would definitely see it coming.

"Oh, my Goodddd," the fiend replied along with a lengthy sigh. "What I gotta do now? Suck yo' dick or some?" She asked. "Come on brah, damn."

Before BM could even tell her what the objective was, she was already sitting down beside him reaching for his pants zipper.

"Oh! Hold on shawty!" BM grabbed her hand and removed it from his dick area. "Naw, that ain't what we on. I need you to do some else for me."

"Oh… aight. What you talking about then nigga?" She was confused.

"Don't be too obvious," BM advised. "But you see that black car, parked over there on P Street?"

The fiend looked slowly in that direction. Cutting her eye to get a quicker look. "Yeah, I see it. What about it though?" She became curious.

"I need you to go pull up on it and see who the fuck up in there. That ma'fucka been sitting right there all day. I ain't even seen nobody get in or out that bitch. I'm startin' to get the feeling that someone is laying on me."

"What?" She asked almost too jokingly for BM liking. "My nigga, yo' ass big tripping. You that paranoid that you think somebody gone take the time to watch yo' ass all day? Besides, if they were smart for real, they'll be tryna stay away from yo' retarded ass."

"I'll give you two dimes," BM offered.

"I'll be right back," she said in a haste about to stand up to get her feet moving.

"Hold up," BM stopped her by grabbing her arm sitting her back down on the porch. "You can't just walk straight up to the car, stupid. I just said I think they watching me. If they laying on me, then they definitely gone see you coming."

"Aight, so how you want me to do it then?" She awaited an answer.

"Come on." Was all BM said as he stood up and went into Tisha's apartment through the back door.

"Maine brah, dis nigga ain't moved all fuckin day," Lil One said still sitting in the passenger seat of the rental. He was quickly growing agitated from remaining stagnant for so long.

"Shidd, that's good." Crow calmly tried to convince his partner. "I ain't tryna be chasing no nigga around all day anyway. Bad enough we gotta baby sit dis grown ass nigga." Crow was unraveling the leaf of a Backwood.

"Oh shit, look," Lil One said. "He taking the junkie bitch in the crib with 'em." Crow laughed. "Nigga bout to get him some head or some."

"He probably bout to fuck the shit out that bitch. Her broke ass must not have no money." Lil One assumed. He was only halfway right though.

"He better, as long as he been sitting right there talking to the bitch," Crow stated. "Shidd… I know I would. No bullshit."

101

"Yo' dirty dick ass be fuckin anything. I'm surprised yo' shit ain't caught on fire yet." Lil One joked with a historical laugh.

"The only reason I ain't caught no STD yet, is cuz yo' mama ain't let me get in that pussy yet nigga." Crow was now laughing twice as hard as Lil One previously was.

"Fuck you nigga!" Lil One said no longer laughing. "Hurry the fuck up and roll that weed up." Lil One was so hot inside from his friends reply, that he forgot that he was still breaking up the weed in a folded dollar bill.

"Naw for real though." Crow tried his best to act as if he was serious. But was barely able to control his laughter. "I heard that pussy so good, that I wouldn't even give a fuck if that shit was burning. I'm still jumping in that ma'fucka. I'm talking 'bout raw dog and all."

Lil One swung a quick backhand over to Crow striking him in his chest. "Aye brah, stop fucking playing with me fo' real. I would try yo' mama but the bitch so ugly, a nigga dick won't even get hard." This type of play was nothing new to the two. It happened all the time every now and then. The real truth was that they loved each other mother's as if they were their own.

"Aight brah, my bad." Crow apologized, still chuckling lightly. "And don't be talking shit 'bout my mama like that. Hurry up and break the weed up, damn."

"I am, nigga. Don't be fuckin rushing me my nig—"

Knock. Knock. Knock.

Lil One spilled some of the weed out of the dollar bill. It fell all over the seat and floor of the car, causing him to look down out of natural instinct.

"What the fuck?" Crow yelled as he grabbed the pistol from beside his seat forgetting all about the Backwood that was in his hand. "Who the fuck is that?"

Crow's question placed Lil One back on point. Saying fuck the weed, he grabbed the gun from his lap and pointed it at the window. "It's that fiend ass bitch that was just in there with BM," Lil One stated the obvious.

"That nigga on us fool." Crow concluded.

"I'm 'bout to smoke dis bitch." Lil One warned Crow.

"What nigga? For what?"

"Cuz fool, if he sent her then she gon' go back and tell that nigga something that's gonna make him come at us his damn self. And if he see who we are with his own eyes, it'll be hard for us to get our free bands every day."

"True. But if he we kill the bitch right here, we gon' make shit hot." Crow was trying to get Lil One to think ahead.

"So," Lil One stated carelessly with a hunch from his shoulders. "All they know is the car fool. We can change that up and park in another spot to watch him from a distance."

Crow thought for a good second. "Aight. Roll yo' window down," he said. "See what the bitch want. What type of game she tryna run."

"What's up?" Lil One asked once the window was low enough to be spoken through. "What you want?"

"Umm…" The fiend slightly stuttered. "Y'all got some work?" She was nervous.

"Bitch did you just—" Lil One had started to snap.

"Yeah," Crow sliced Lil One's sentence in half. "Get in. We got you."

Reluctantly, the fiend opened the back door to the rental and climbed into the backseat. Immediately, Crow locked all the doors and pulled away from the curb with excessive speed. Lil One turned the gun towards the backseat and aimed it at the joining passenger. He climbed fully in the back and took a seat beside her. "Look, I jus—" She started to say, but couldn't finish her words because they were stopped.

"Listen here, bitch," Lil One spoke. Ain't nobody tryna hear none of them bullshit as lies yo' ass bout to spit out yo' dirty ass mouth." He violently grabbed her by the jaw and poked the gun in her face. "Now, tell me exactly why yo' ass came over to dis muthafucking car fucking with a nigga?"

"I'm just tryna get high." The fiend half lied, and half told the truth.

"Oh yeah?" Lil One questioned. "So, you tellin' me that you willing to lose yo' life over some fucking get high?"

"You know it don't get no higher than heaven, right?" Crow commented in the form of a question. Followed by a laugh that would've gave the devil chills.

"Oh naw. Dis bitch going straight to hell. Right along with the rest of us."

"Please, don't kill me. I'll do whatever y'all want me to do. Jus Please don't kill me!" The woman begged. But her words went to two pairs of death ears.

"Aight bitch." Lil One shoved her face towards the window. Her head banged up against it. With her right hand, she rubbed head on the aching spot. "We can cut all the games out." Lil One continued. "And you gone tell us exactly why the fuck that nigga BM sent you over to this car." Lil One stopped talking exactly one second before he talked again. "And yo' ass better not fucking lie. Because we saw yo' dumb ass over there talking to the nigga the whole fuckin time." Lil One put it all on the table. It was no way she could even think about lying.

"Them drugs got you so fucked up, that you let that nigga use you like a fucking pawn. He walked you right into yo' grave. And you was to blind to even see it coming." Crow added in as he drove through the darkness of the night.

"Okay. Oh... kay," A tear had begun to roll down the woman's cheek. She was only twenty-nine years old, which was fairly still kind of young depending on the way one lived their life. At that moment, she had started to regret the waisted years of her life. She wondered how it even got this far from the beginning. How did she allow something that she intended to only be a one-time thing, happen over and over a thousand times plus. In some strange silently knowing way, she knew this was it. She wished like hell that yesterday could have been her last day of using the drugs that she had come accustomed to abuse.

Hell, she wished that she'd never had a first day at all. Now, she knew exactly where that day had led her to. Still, even with knowing, she remained hopeful.

"I was a lil short—" the lady stopped herself from talking before she continued "Well, basically all I had was four dollars…" If these were her last moments of life, she'd rather go out an Honest Abe. Hopefully, her last moments of truth would be just enough to get her through the gates of heaven. "Like I said, I was just tryna get high. So, BM told me that he would give me a lil some extra jus to come over here and see who was in the car. Thats it, I swear that was all. He just wanted me to see who y'all was sitting in the car." She tried to sniff up the tears that had cried down her face. Leaning her head against the window, she cried a silent prayer.

"How the fuck he even know we was laying on him?" Crow asked out loud, though not to either one of the passengers in particular.

"He didn't." The fiend volunteered the information. "Well, he did. But he wasn't sure. Thats why he sent me."

"So, he just sent you to see who we was?" Crow wanted to know. This time directing his question particularly at her.

"Yes. That's the only reason."

"So, what was he gon' do once you told him?" Crow continued his questioning.

"I'on know. He didn't tell me none of that. All he told me to do was go out the front door and walk round the back of the projects so y'all wouldn't notice that I was coming. See who, if anybody was in the car and let him know."

"That nigga on our line."

"Yeah, but I think she telling the truth though," Lil One spoke.

I think so too. But, if we send her back, how do we know if we can trust her." Crow wondered.

"What you mean?"

Lil One's words were sharp. "We can't trust her ass. We don't even know this bitch. This could be the nigga aunt or some. We don't know."

"I swear, I won't say shit!" The fiend promised. "Or y'all can make up some shit for me to go back and tell 'em. But if y'all don't hurt me. I swear—"

"Shut up bitch!" The two juveniles yelled at the woman at the same time. "You can save that shit." Lil One continued. "If you go back tellin' that nigga you don't know nothing after he seen you getting in the car with us, he gone kill you his damn self. And if you go back spitting that lying ass bullshit, he definitely gone kill you. Just because he gon' think you was tryna set him up." Crow drove the car down to Shockoe Bottom, the canal walk section. Slowly, he crept the car down a dirt road that lead to a wooden area. All was silent like the night before Christmas. The lights went off and the total darkness was turned on.

"What you wanna do with dis bitch bro? I'm tired of playing and shit."

"You think we should call Keem?" Crow suggested.

"For what? That nigga find out we fucked this up, he might fire our asses," Lil One said basically denying the suggestion. "You heard what he said, niggas already wanna take our spot."

"Yeah brah, but if we try to cover this shit up, it's gon' make us look disloyal and untrustworthy. Shit, basically we ain't do none wrong. We did what the nigga told us to do. Plus, that's what he gave us the phone for in the first place.

"Wait, y'all workin for Keem?" The woman asked in total awe. Of course, she knew of Keem. He was a neighborhood hero all over the city.

"Shut the fuck up!" The two yelled again. "Aye, look bitch, you speak again without us tellin' you to, I'ma torture yo' ass out this bitch all fuckin night until the sun come up."

Lil One gave her promising threat placing the pistol back into her face.

"Give me the phone, brah," Crow ordered. "I'ma call him, fuck it. Let 'em know what's goin' on and see what he want us to do." Without protest, Lil One tossed the phone into the front seat, landing it in Crow's lap. He picked it up and rung the line to the other burner phone. It rung all the way through before going to voicemail. He tried again and got the same result. He attempted it a third time, but this time wasn't a charm.

"Nigga ain't answerin' that ma'fucka fool."

"What the fuck the nigga give us a phone fo' if he ain't gone answer?" Lil One asked a million-dollar question.

"No bullshit," Crow agreed. "Got a nigga blowin' up the phone like I'm his bitch or some." At the end of Crow's sentence, the phone he held in his hand started to ring back. "Yoo," he answered on the first ring.

"Yeah," Keem replied from the other end of the phone. He had the voice of a man who had just been awaken from out of his sleep.

"Yeah, big brah we—" Before Crow could fully complete his statement, he was distracted by a woman going off in Keem's background.

"So, who the fuck is it Hakeem?"

She was loud and obnoxious with a tone of voice that was expressed with anger. It was his baby mother. "Yo ass think you so slick. What the fuck you need with two phones?" Keem didn't resist. He never returned a word to her. He easily allowed her to snatch the phone from out of his hands. "Hello!" She yelled through the receiver.

"Yo," Crow said already over the baby mama drama that he had nothing to do with. Shit, the little nigga ain't even have kids. So, it's understandable for him not to understand.

"Who the fuck is dis?" Keem's baby mama asked still yelling, although deep down inside she felt dumb as hell to hear a male's voice reply back to her.

"This Mike," Crow lied. After all, it was a burner phone for a reason.

"Oh," the baby mama replied. "What you want?" she asked a question, even she knew was stupid. Crow chuckled but didn't answer. Not wanting to say Keem's name directly over the phone.

"Thank you," Keem said as he removed the phone from her hand. "I appreciate you waking me up too by the way." Although he seemed sarcastic, he was sincerely being genuine.

"Aight... my bad," she said shamefully.

"What's up brah?" Keem got back to the conversation that technically never got started. "My bad 'bout that."

"Naw, you good. But we gotta problem."

"Talk to me."

"Dude on to us. He even sent somebody at us."

"What you mean?"

"He know we watching him. Well, he don't know it's us, but he sent somebody to see what was up and... well, we basically kidnapped them."

Keem laughed nonchalantly, "Aight so what?"

"Me and brah debating on if we should—"

"Naw, y'all know what to do," Keem assured seriously. "It's not up for debate. After y'all handle that, fall back for the night. Get up with me in the AM and I'ma put some different shoes on y'all feet." By shoes Keem meant wheels, which meant changing up cars.

"Aight bet." Crow understood. "Say no more." And the phone call was ended.

"Well, my nigga," Crow said to Lil One. "Looks like it's time to party."

"Shidd, I'm down. What song we dancing to?" Lil had threw an arm in the air and started dancing. Bopping around like the rapper Da Baby in the backseat of the car.

"Shidd…" Crow shook his head looking out the window at the flow of the James River. "It looks like 'Wait In The Water.'" He announced.

Lil One got stuck in motion at the title of the song. "Aw, thats fucked up." He admitted. "But I like it though." He admitted again. "Make it look like she drowned or some. And we can save a bullet or two."

"Yeah, all that." Crow agreed. "Aye, you still got that eight ball on you?" He asked referring to an eighth of an ounce of crack that Lil One had since this morning.

"You know I do fool." He answered. "What, you gone let her go out in style?"

"Yeah brah." Crow sounded a little down about the situation. "We gon' let her go out with a bang."

"Shidd… we might as well get some pussy too while we at it. Make dis shit a party for real." Lil One half joked, as he pulled the drug from his pocket.

"And talking about I'm the one with the dirty dick. Come on man, so we can get dis shit out the way." Crow was opening the driver's side door on his way out the car.

"Aye look," Lil One said to the fiend. "We gon' try to make dis as easy as possible. Just don't make it hard for us, aight."

The woman shook her head with a yes as streams of tears flowed down her face like a river heading down stream. "Aight, let's go." By this time, Crow was at the back side of the passenger door, opening it, making sure she didn't make a run for it.

Without force, she got out of the car and walked in the middle of the kids. The woman cried as if she was heading down the aisle at a funeral. It was like she was approaching her own casket. "Waiit, in the water. Waiit in the water children. Waiit in the water—"

"Maine shut the fuck up!" Crow snapped at the immatureness of Lil One. "Keep singing that dumb ass shit."

"Oh my bad. Shit, You picked the song." Lil One reminded. The three of them walked to the end of a dock that oversaw one of the deepest ends of the James River.

"Go ahead. Sit down," Crow told the woman in tears."

"Huh?" The woman asked in confusion.

"Sit down," he said again a little more sternly. He was telling her to sit at the edge of the deck. Even though it scared her, it scared her even more to see what would happen if she didn't.

"Here." Lil One handed the woman the eight ball of crack cocaine. "Hope you got yo' works, cuz I'on sell that type of shit. She took the drugs without a word.

Afterwards, she pulled her lighter and crack pipe from her pockets. Once the rock was on the stem, she added the flame from the lighter. As the crack melted on the pipe, the woman's heart and soul melted along with it. Lil One and Crow stood by as they watched the lady smoke rock after rock back-to-back.

"We might not have to kill her ass ourselves. She about to kill her damn self." Lil One predicted. The flow of the tears from the fiend's eyes had stopped coming. She stared out over the river in a daze, listening to the sounds of splashing water. She was so high that she just sat with a half of gram remaining in her hand as if she forgot it was ever there. Crow looked over at Lil One who read his mind as easy as a Dr. Suess book. Together using a foot a piece, they kicked her off the edge of the dock. Her body splashed face first into the cold water. For a few seconds, her body floated as if she was already deceased. Then suddenly, she started flopping and splashing, struggling to gain control of her body. Lil One aimed his pistol towards her preparing to take a shot.

"Hold on," Crow suggested stretching his arm out. The woman's body dipped beneath the water. Bubbles surfaced on the top of the water. "You know black people can't swim."

Crow informed his friend. Desperate for a breath of air, the woman's body shot back up above the water.

"Oh shit," Lil One jumped back a little. Not expecting it to happen. "Maine, I'm about to shoot this bitch."

Crow laughed. "Naw, she goin' back under. Jus wait." As his words traveled through the air, the woman had took her last breath of air. She took one big gasp right before the water pulled her back underneath, similar to the drugs she was hooked on. The two boys waited for a minute to see if she would pop back up. She never did.

"Waiit in the water… waiit in the water children… waiit—" Lil One had begun to sing the negro spiritual that Harriet Tubman used to guide the slaves to freedom. Guess it was safe to say, the woman was now free.

"Nigga! Shut the fuck up!" Crow shouted agitated in a low tone of voice. "Come on mane. We gotta go get some more weed. Yo' scary ass dropped all the gas all over the floor."

"No bullshit," Lil One agreed. "Nigga need to get high after this shit." They made their way back to the car. "Hold up, nigga. It's my turn to drive." Lil One stopped crow from getting behind the wheel. Crow handed the keys over with a sigh and headed around to the passenger's side.

LESSON 1.14
Stand Tall

Knock. Knock. Knock.

"Um Foster!" The C.O. yelled in the cell door after knocking on the door three times. "Foster! Do you want your meds?"

It was a new day. The C.O.'s had changed shifts. The sound of the woman's voice caused E to open his eyes. "You need to get up right quick. The nurse need to see you for yo' treatment.

At the opening of his eyes, E's body was washed over with a rush of pain. Even muscles that he'd never felt before ached. Immediately, he wished that he'd never woke up at that moment. Wished that he could at least sleep one more day away. Maybe the pain would disappear by then. Not only was his body in pain, but his pride was as well. It was crushed the very moment he laid eyes on the steal sink that was connected to the steel toilet. Then, it all came pouring into his mind like the flood in the days of Noah. The place he was at. The tier he was on. The fights of last night. The stressful flights in the hospital. Him getting shot by his best friend. Ike and Ron getting killed. The shootout in the store. The robbery. It all put him a state of desperation.

"Come on," The woman C.O said once she realized that E was laying there awoke. "Let's go get you taken care of. And then you can come back in here and lay down if you want to." Her voice was the sweetest thing E had heard all year. Well, actually for a long time for that matter. Even though he knew that all the nurse would do was barely the bare minimum, she still spoke as if she cared.

Somehow, E found the strength to lift his head up and turn it towards the door. His neck felt tight and heavy. The pain made him want to remain laying. "You, okay?" The C.O asked concerned. "Can you get up?"

"Yeah," E may have spoken to soon. Because he was actually unsure himself. Although, his pride was hurt from being in such a weak predicament, he refused to let a woman that he didn't even know, see him as such. He used his arms first to slowly peel his torso off the mat.

"Thats it." The C.O. encouraged genuinely. "There you go. Take your time." With the knuckles of his fist planted on the floor, he pushed and found the leverage he needed to climb up off his knees. The C.Os of the jail had suspicion of the fight but absolutely no proof. So the woman had no idea about the pain he was in. She couldn't even imagine it. All she knew was that she admired the strength that she witnessed at this moment. E placed a hand on the wall for balance. He stood tall before turning around to face the woman in the doorway. "You ready now?" She asked.

Her hair was all hers. It dropped about two inches past her shoulders with curls dangling. A few curls wrapped around her acorn complexioned neck. The only thing there was tattoo that read Tiara, and a golden necklace that was tucked underneath her uniform. Her edges were in total control. Her eyebrows were thick but arched precisely. Her lashes were thick and long. He eyes dark brown and clear. Her cheekbones were slightly high. Her jaw line was sort of wide. They came together perfectly causing two dimples to kiss each side of her face. Her nose was as cute as a button. Her lips, seductively sexy. Her teeth were as pearl white as the gates to heaven and aligned like perfectly stacked bricks. She stood 5' 6" about 160 lbs. with 34-28- 40 measurements that could be seen through her uniform. Nails done and mostly likely toes too. E wondered why the hell she was working in a place like this. Regardless of why, he was happy that she did for his sake. And oddly enough, he was happy to be there to see her.

"Yeah," E replied to her question that seemed to be asked so long ago. "I'm ready." He tried to take a step and damn near fell. He stumbled, attempting to get his feet up underneath him. Grabbing hold of the sink, he looked up into the mirror and took a quick look at himself. He went from admiring beauty to staring at a beast. He had a lump on his forehead that was visible with enough focus. One under his left eye that was clear as day. And his lips was swollen. Dried up blood still rested on his bottom lip. He pushed the button on the sink and ran water over it, to wash it away.

"What happened to you?" The C.O wanted to know.

"Shit, for real." E brushed off. "Got into a fight before I got shot. Thats all." He lied, making his way to the door.

"Umm-hmm," she said as she took a step back giving him room to walk out the cell. As he exited the cell, E stopped. He read her name tag and the name Crawford. From there he assumed her name to be Tiara Crawford. He stuck his left hand toward the direction that they should be headed in. He was being generous and genius. For real though, he didn't need to see her backside in order to know that she was dragging a wagon.

"You think you slick," Crawford said with a corner of her lip turning up into a half smile. "Boy go head." Then, she giggled.

With light limps, due to the tightness of his legs, E lead the way through the tier. Just as they were last night, all eyes were on him. Unknowingly, he had earned the respect of most because of his brave heart. Even a few of his enemies respected the fact that he was able to stand tall all on his own and without a weapon. To the true soldiers, that spoke loud enough to bring down the walls of Jericho. Not only had he threw down with the fist, but he stuck around, and didn't snitch.

The whispers still buzzed through the air. But the choice of words were different. "Naw, that nigga go hard."

"Yeah, I'll give 'em his props."

"Them niggas had to bank him."

"Dude probably smoke all them niggas when he hit that land."

"Shidd... it ain't ova watch. He gone take off on somebody before the day over."

As best as he tried to ignore the whispers, it was damn near impossible. At certain times, he wanted to scream out loud and tell everyone to just shut the fuck up. But he knew he would be viewed as a psycho.

The nurse had changed the gauze to his wounds and gave him a couple Tylenol threes to help him endure the pain. She asked him was he okay. He said he was good and that was that. E turned from the chuck hole that was right at the C.O.'s station. "You did all that for that?" E nonchalantly asked Crawford. Really, he didn't care. He was happy that she did. Even though the Tylenol threes wasn't a 30mg Percocet, he figured if they could rid him of at least a percentage of the pain. He'd be grateful and strong enough to handle the rest. Besides all of that, he was really asking for the sake of conversation.

"It looked like you needed them," she said wisely. "And plus, I'm just doing my job." The look she gave him challenged his nerve to be so ungrateful.

Starring into her bold and brown beautiful eyes, E saw nothing but truth. "You know what?" He asked as a matter of fact. "You right." He agreed, changing up the angle to his approach now that he had gotten a small taste of her personality. "I should be saying thank you. I appreciate that."

C.O Crawford scanned her eyes over E's light brown skin complexion. His eyes were a shade above the hazel color as if they were mixed with a tear drop of honey. His waves were thick and shiny even at its roughest stage. It resembled the ocean in the middle of a thunderstorm. With all the scars and bruises on E's face, he had all the signs of a bad boy. Yet, he had the sex appeal of a pretty boy. At that moment, Tiara Crawford remembered why she had chosen that job. "Well," she said attempting her best to seem unimpressed. "Even though you don't have to thank me, I'll still give you a welcome."

They stared at each other for a silent moment. E was trying to figure out what he wanted to say next. He just couldn't figure it out. Actually, he was doing exactly what it was that he wanted to do. That was, soak up her beauty.

"Don't do that," Crawford said snapping out of the love gaze. "Thats weird."

"What?" He asked acting confused.

"Staring like that," she replied. "Why you doing that?"

"Why wouldn't I?" He asked as to say, it's obvious. She smiled. "You called me weird." He reminded her of her own words from only a few seconds ago.

"Aww... did I offend you?" She asked as if she was talking to a little baby. "You want me to say I'm sorry?"

"No," E replied dryly. "You know what weird means?"

"Umm... yeah," she sarcastically said now feeling offended herself. "But do you wanna tell me something that I already knew?"

"It means different," he shot out. "So, if being weird could make me different from all of this, then, I guess I'd rather be weird." He released a sigh after finishing his sentence. "I'm tired of this shit," he mumbled to himself as he put his head down on his arms that were folded on the C.O horseshoe shaped desk.

"Once again Crawford was able to see the struggle between pain and strength. "You wanna go lay back down?" She asked for two reasons. "Cuz if so you need to go ahead now, so I can close that door. I have to go out for a few."

"Naw I'm good." E lifted his head up and looked around the tier. "I need to get on the phone anyway."

"Okay, well, don't get in no trouble before I get back." E sensed a hint of flirt. Though, it was hard to tell because he felt as if every woman should want him. He was most right most of the time.

"Naw, I ain't gone do that." He sounded certain but was truly unsure. "I wanna make sure I'll be able to see you again."

Crawford smiled but tried her best to conceal it. "Well, I'll definitely be back." Without another word, she turned to face the door jiggling her keys as she did. She used them to let herself off the tier. E stood there for confirmation. Him and other nigga watched as she headed to the second door. Her ass was round, slightly wide with perfect cuffs. She had a gap in between her legs that was out of view of the tier. She looked towards E with a slanted eye for confirmation herself. As she already knew, he was watching her wagging.

Once she was gone, E unexpectedly turned to face the tier. It was approximately ten o'clock in the morning. Around the same time that most of the tier was just starting to wake up.

"Aye!" He yelled out shutting up everyone's conversations and stopping everyone's movements. "I'ma tell y'all niggas straight up. I ain't checking off no ma'thafuckin tier. So, if y'all niggas want me gone, you gone have to be ready to rumble everyday up in dis bitch! Unless one of y'all police ass niggas try to drop a kite on a nigga. Or hit me with the PREA."

A few niggas laughed at the last remark. E ignored it and continued, "As far as that shit that happened last night, when it comes to Pound and Taz, I'ma respect y'all gangsta." A lot of niggas were confused. They could not understand E's wisdom behind his approach. It was mainly because they were clueless to what he was going through at that moment. The same nigga that he had placed his life on the line with. The same nigga he had stood side by side with creating the same enemies that he was now confronting alone, was the same nigga that tried to kill him. All had E thinking differently. His near-death experience was an eye opener to the door of intelligence. From now on, he would put them over his emotions.

"And for y'all bitch ass niggas that banked me," his voice was raised a little higher. "I'ma let that shit slide. But if anybody else on this tier tryna see me, we can shoot the one right now. Cuz anything after this, I'm taking all beef to the streets. And I'm pretty sure all y'all niggas know how I gets down out that bitch. Shit gets ten times worse. Trust me."

For a minute, no one said a word, until,

"Shidd, I want my one," a nigga said coming from standing in front of the TV. E knew exactly who it was. "What's up?" His named was D-Roc. He was from the top of Mosby Court Projects and grew up on Reed Street. It was an inner hood beef that ended with D-Roc's cousin being murdered right before his eyes. "Nigga you know what the fuck it is."

"Aye look, stickman, I ain't kill yo' people, brah." E already knew what the animosity was about. "But we can definitely shoot the one if you feel some type of way."

"Nigga I ain't yo' stickman or yo' brotha. And even if you didn't, then yo' homeboy did and that's one in the same. So let's go!" D-Roc was making his way into the bathroom, where he and E would rumble it out at out of cameras sight. There was no hesitation in his step as E walked into the bathroom. The door swung like one of those old doors would when walking into a bar in the Wild West. Compacted in the small space, they immediately went to throwing fist. Out of the bathroom, the sounds of stomping feet and fist pounding faces with loud smacks could be heard.

For a good thirty-five seconds it was blow for blow in the battle. With one block and a hard counter punch, E was able to gain a slight edge in the battle. That was until D-Roc having the heavier frame got a hold of E's body and slammed it to the floor of the bathroom. He pinned E down with his body and used his hands to smoosh his face into the floor.

"Yall niggas killed my fucking cuzin." Tears were starting to slide down his face from his eyes. "My fuckin cuzin."

For the first time, E felt some type of remorse for ever having something to do with taking away a person's family member. Even though he was telling the truth, he still felt partly responsible. "Brah, I ain't claming no bodies I ain't drop," E mustered to mumble underneath the pressure D-Roc applied to his face. "If I had did it nigga, I'll wear it. The fuck I got to gain from lying? Ducking a fight, I'ma fight anyway?" What E said made plenty of sense to D-Roc. He felt a little better getting some of the hatred off his chest. But, the rest he would save for the one who really deserved it.

D-Roc got up off E and helped him off the ground. Respectfully, they dapped up and even embraced for a hot second or two. They both had words on their tongue that they wanted to speak. But they allowed the silence to provide all the understanding that they needed. Together, they exited the bathroom as if everything was normal. "Aye, nigga let me get next on one of them phones." E requested.

LESSON 1.15
Expect The Unexpected

"Aight look, give me the two hundred fifty dollars now, and I'll have the Js Friday." Derek was behind the counter at the cash register talking to one of his favorite customers. The man he spoke to went into his pockets preparing to pull out the money requested. "Hold up nigga!" Derek stopped him with haste. "You know it's camera's fool. I can't be seen takin money from you without you buyin' some. Jus hit the Cashapp."

"Oh yeah. You right. My bad, D." The man raised his hand above the counter and reached over towards Derek to give him a dap.

"It's all good fool. I'll hit you Friday when them joints come in."

"Bet," the customer said. He turned around and headed towards the door. As he was leaving out, two more customers were coming in.

"Good afternoon," Derek called out to the two. "If y'all need any help just let me know." He offered his service. The man looked at Derek with a mischievous smirk on his face. Derek felt a wicked vibe from the man's energy.

"Thank you," the woman said as her and the man traveled to the woman's shoe section.

The couple was Tank and Shawndra. Before today, Shawndra never really noticed Derek. Little did she know, the whole time, their hearts shared the same pains.

Shawndra pulled out her phone and sent a text to Kadesha telling her to call ASAP. "You don't wanna get you a pair of shoes or an outfit?" She asked Tank trying to get some space in between them.

"Yeah," Tank replied. "I'ma go ova here to check some shit out." She knew Tank loved to dress fresh with the latest.

Shawndra's phone rung at a perfect timing. She answered on the first ring. "Bitch." She basically whispered through the phone. "You said the nigga was fine," she said speaking of Derek. "But you definitely forgot the other fine. Cuz bitch the nigga is fine fine."

"Gurl, I told yo' ass." Kadesha replied. "Where the fuck you at?"

"At DTLR duhh." Shawndra picked up a pair of shoes as if she was interested.

"Bitch you better get that nigga number while you in there."

"I can't, hoe," Shawndra explained.

"And tell me why... da... fuck... not?" Kadesha dragged out her words.

"Because." Shawndra started to say, She looked around to make sure that Tank wasn't around her or in ear shot. "Tank ass in here with me."

"Uhh bitch," Kadesha instigated. "You better watch that sneaky ass nigga," she warned.

"For what though?"

"Cuz that sneak a link probably know exactly who the fuck that man is while he putting dick all up in his bitch the whole time." Her words made Shawndra think long and hard.

"You know what?" Shawndra agreed. "You right." The thought of Tank cheating put her in a whole different mind frame. She looked over at Tank who was shuffling through a rack of shirts. "I'ma call you later."

For the rest of their time in the store Shawndra watched Tank closely. She was looking for any indication that he knew Derek. She picked out a pair of Air Max 95's and was ready to go.

"Umm… excuse me," she said to Derek. "Can you get these for me in a size six please?"

"I'll be right over," Derek replied.

As soon as Derek stepped from behind the counter, Tank was on the way to meeting him at Shawndra's side. He tried to wrap his arm around her. "Yes size six please. Thank you."

"Got you" Derek took the shoe. "I'll be right back." The couple awaited a minute in silence. Derek came back out with the two shoes in a box. "If you ready, I can take 'em over. Here go you miss."

"Naw that ain't it," Tank butted in. He picked up a random shoe that he only half liked. "I need these in a nine and a half." Tank removed the shoebox out of Derek's hand and handed him the single shoe. Derek looked at him a bit confused. He felt that for some reason Tank was purposely being funny. He just didn't understand why. Regardless, he still had a job to do. Derek returned this time in less than a minute. "This one too," Tank said meeting Derek with another shoe. Derek did what he was getting paid to do. But there was no way to avoid noticing the mockery in Tank's actions. So did Shawndra. It was evident that Tank definitely knew who Derek was.

Derek came back out with the third shoebox in hand. "Here you go. Anything else I could help y'all with?" Derek asked cheerfully. When he was in the back, he had a moment to think to himself. While Tank was being a dickhead, Derek was racking up sells. Plus, he concluded that Tank must have been hating on him for some reason. Maybe, he was jealous of something that he had. Whatever it was, he wouldn't allow it to stress him.

"Nope," Tank said childishly. He took the other two shoeboxes and piled them on the one that Derek had in his hand. "That'll be all, shoe boy." Derek ignored the shade and made his way over to the cash register.

"Do y'all have a DTLR membership card?" Derek asked.

"Umm... yeah," Shawndra answered.

"Can I have the phone number to it please?"

"804-204..."

"Okay. Thank you. The total will be five-hundred thirty-six and seventy-eight cent please." Tank pulled out a roll of bills that was 'bout five to six thousand dollars. He peeled off five-hundred and handed it to Derek.

"I won't all my change back too."

"No problem," Derek said as he handed off the money. Tank stuffed the money in his pocket and walked away without even bothering to grab one of the bags. "Wish I can help you," Derek said to make sure not to be heard by Tank.

"You can," Shawndra whispered as she snatched the bags off the table. "Use that number and I'll tell you how." Derek watched as Shawndra walked out of the store. Her words kind of threw him for a loop. That was until he looked at the computer number in the system. That had to be what she meant by using the number. Maybe Shawndra had the answers to why Tank disliked him so much. There was only one way to find out.

***

Mac stood looking over the city through condo windows with his hands behind his back. "I promised you an opportunity to take yo' game to the next level. And now that chance has come. Me and..." Mac paused for a few. "Well, let's just say a few friends of mine, decided to try you out. You should know by now. But, whenever one's status rises it usually comes with a few more responsibilities." Mac was making the situation seem more important than it was. Then again, depending on how you looked at it, it was. This was Keem's chance to prove himself. He was under a microscopic light. One that would definitely burn him if he made the wrong decision or move.

"Your focus needs to be laser bean sharp. You need to let yo' team know that it's up for twenty twenty-four. Let 'em know that you've established yourself. Giving them an opportunity to eat off a bigger table with more food on its plate."

Keem loved the talk. He was just anxious to find out what Mac's lengthy elaboration was about. He sat cool as if he had his thoughts in control. To be honest though, they were racing at light years speed. The one thing that he had no problem with was the challenge. He loved to be tested. It was the feeling of going through the challenge that finish line. What better feeling was there then crossing the line with a victory. That same victorious feeling was the very same high he yearned for. That feeling was the reason he never took his money and went the slow legit route. It was the same reason he always looked to get deeper and deeper into the game. He was addicted like the very fiends his crew served.

"Aye Chop, the luggage." Mac ordered. Chop and his righthand walked into the living room carrying a bag in each hand. They laid them at the feet of Keem. Mac turned around and faced Keem. "Thats twenty bricks. It's the same number times five. I'ma tell you this. You will be faced with an obstacle. Though I can't tell you exactly what that may be, that's only because it's part of yo' test. Aside from that, you won't be able to call me for shit. I'm goin' on vacation. In two weeks, I'll contact you and you should be ready by then. Oh yeah and one more thing, whatever you do, show love to Them Ward niggas. It's mandatory."

Keem was escorted out of the condominiums with more bricks than he'd ever had all at once. And he had two weeks to move it. He wasn't worried as all. He thought about the big boost of paper he'd have in the next two weeks, and it excited him more than the bitches in Magic City did.

LESSON 1.16
Don't Play

The unexpected meeting with Mac made Keem almost forget about the baby-sitting mission on BM. He had to get the bricks straight to the spot. And he needed to get the youngins back around Mosby so they could get their eye's back on BM. There were only one person that could really help him right now. Even though he hated to dial the number, he did so anyway. Besides, it was only a small favor he was asking for.

"Lil brah."

"Yo," Shy said over the phone.

"I need you fool," Keem reluctantly replied.

"I knew the time would come," Shy said with a confident humble reply. "What's good, big brah? I got you."

"I need you to get them lil niggas and switch up the rental and make sure they ass back out Mosby ASAP."

"Aight shidd, say no more. Thats some small. But was really good though? Them lil niggas fumbled the ball, huh?"

"Naw, not really." Keem went to change up the topic. "Aye, you got a band on you until I get up wit you?"

"You already know I do, fool. Why, what's up?"

"Aight. Give it to them two fools and I'ma hit yo' hand when I run into you."

"Aight brah. I'ma take care of it," Shy assured. "You good though?"

"Yeah, errthing gucci. I ain't gone lie though, a nigga hands kinda full right now, my nigga. Shit getting real out this bitch." Keem was highly excited. Not knowing that his energy was lifting Shy to his frequency. He was unknowingly making Shy fiend for the exact same high that he was on.

"Already, already," Shy said dryly as if he didn't give a fuck. But really, he was disappointed cause he was forced to take the dry route in life. Ever since he could remember he's been sheltered from the very same streets he was raised in. His father was a hustler. He gave his life to the game. Literary, doing a life sentence in a federal penitentiary. Keem was a hustler and definitely showed no signs of looking to live any life other than that. Even their gun slinging brother Wild Boy had a hustle in his soul before he died, giving his life to the streets. It was clear why they all wanted Shy to remain on the sidewalk. But the two things they were blind too was the fact that they all were hypocrites and that the hustle was running all through his blood. He was a natural born hustler. And after seeing the mistakes that they all made over the last two decades, he studied enough to be one of the best there were. "Where the fuck them lil niggas at?"

"Oh yeah." Keem almost forgot. "I left the phone at my baby mama's house. You can go over there and get it or you can chase they lil ass all over the south. I doubt if they sittin' round Hillside with wheels."

"You'll be surprised. Cuz that's probably exactly what they dumb ass doing. Showing off and shit You know them niggas ain't use to having shit. Call yo' BM though. Let her know I'm on my way to pick that joint up. You might need it later on anyway." Shy was thinking ahead, and Keem noticed the effort.

"Already, I'm about to hit her now and put her on game. Good looking, lil brah. And hit me up when you got then stationed." Keem was happy as hell that he could depend on him at a time when it was needed.

CRIME PAYS | SELF MADE TAY

"Got cha, fool. Gone."

Already. Love you nigga."

"Love you more fool." Shy ended the call and got ready to make his way to the Northside of the city. He stepped out the door in a red and black Jordan sweatsuit with a pair of black and red Jordans 11s. Topped off with Chicago Bulls New Era fitted. That was his favorite team. His ride was an all-black 2022 Hyundai Tucson. It was Range Rover like his brothers whip, but it was clean and loved it like it was a newborn baby. He hopped in and pulled off blasting "7220" the latest from his favorite rapper which was Lil Durk. In fact, he was hooked on Chicago everything from the Bears to the Cubs.

By the time he had pulled up to 1st Avenue, Keem's baby mama was waiting for him on the porch. She walked to the car and handed him the phone. He noticed a look of distress on her face.

"What's up with you? You good?" He asked.

"Yeah, I'm just waiting on Mo's dumb ass. He supposed to be doin' some for me."

"Oh, aight. Tell my niece I said I love her when she get out school." "Okay. I will." She headed back into the house.

Shy sat in the car and dialed the number to the other burner phone.

"what's up lil nigga?" He asked when Lil One answered the phone. "I see y'all lil niggas been blowing the phone up," Shy referred to all the missed calls he saw in the phone. "Y'all good?"

"Yeah, we good," Lil One replied. "Where Keem?" Niggas tryna get back to work."

"Like that about you. Y'all meet me at the airport, now!" Shy ordered.

"Shidd, we on the way now," Lil One said and then challenged Shy. "I betcha we beat you there."

"Naw," Shy denied the race. "Y'all niggas drive like y'all got some sense. Take yo' time. Ain't no need to fuck up errthing up over the speed limit." Shy was wise, and right.

"Already, you right," the youngins said taking heed to Shy's advice.

They got to the airport and swapped out cars. They changed the 2022 Dodge Charger SRT Hellcat Widebody edition which was all black, for a 2022 Toyota RAV4 SUV, same color. It was Shy's idea. After hearing from the pair why they had to change cars, he suggested that his suggestion was a little less flashy. And it blended in a lot more. Beggers couldn't be choosers. So, they didn't complain. Shy gave them their thousand dollar payment and they all made their way to Mosby.

BM hadn't even attempted to change locations. He figured for what? His plan was going exactly as planned. He felt it strange that he didn't see that fiend since she got in that car yesterday. To him it meant nothing. All he knew was that whoever it was watching, had better not come back. Because if so, he'd be all over they ass like a pamper on a newborn.

Shy parked on Mosby Street at a distance from where his eyes were set, which was just directly down the street. He wanted to be sure that his car was not seen. And definitely up close.

"Y'all niggas park a lil up the street so y'all will be able to see 'em. And y'all will be on his blindside as well, instead of being directly in his face."

"Aight brah, we on it," Lil One assured.

"Guess I'ma have the phone for a min. At least until brah call for it. Still though, if y'all niggas need me just hit the line." Shy was already pulling away from the curb, making a left turn on the Martin Luther King Jr.'s bridge.

"Bet. Say no more." The phone conversation ended. "That nigga Shy cool as a bitch for real."

"Yeah, brah aight." Crow agreed.

They sat across the street from Martin Luther King Jr.'s Middle School. That was basically built in the middle of Mosby. The car was partly sheltered by a project building. Around the corner of that building, they had a perfect vision of BM sitting on the porch. Still trapping with the same clothes that he had on yesterday.

"Let me see the light." Lil One threw the Bic lighter over to Crow and placed flame to the twisted Backwood. "Dis nigga boring as a bitch." He inhaled as he spoke on BM.

"No bullshit." Lil One agreed. "Free band gang though. Shidd... I ain't tripping."

BM was sitting on the porch acting as if he was unaware of the presence of the new car that he'd never seen before. With his phone in his lap, he dialed a number. The ringtone rung through the speaker phone. "Kior, and Bianca ready?"

"Yeah, brah," Kiora said over the phone. "You want us to go now?"

"Yeah. Go head, make it happen. It's that all black Toyota truck parked on Mosby Street."

"We got you, brah."

The plan was already mapped out. Kiora had a Bluetooth earbud in one of her ears. Her and Bianca walked out of the Jefferson Townhouse's. They headed down Mosby Street, on the opposite side where Lil One and Crow were parked. They both sported a pair of leggings that showed off all their curves from the waist down. Kiora's was pink. Bianca's white. The two eighteen years of age girls walked passed the school paying no mind to the car across the street.

Lil One looked passed Crow who was leaning back in the seat reclining. "Damn! Look at them two lil bitches." Lil One spotted first bringing the pair to Crow's awareness. On instinct, he looked up and took a glance out the window.

"Damn!" Crow cried. "That joint in the pink phat as a bitch."

"Shidd... both of them bitches phat. The fuck you talking about?" Lil One reached over to the wheel and beeped the horn at the girls. They looked back through the car's window but waved the boys off nonchalantly.

"Yeah, it's two boys in the car," Kiora said through the earpiece.

"Who the fuck is it?" BM asked. "Yall know the niggas?"

"Hell naw," Kiora said.

"I ain't never seen them niggas," Bianca said in the background.

"Stuck up ass bitches," Crow said watching as the two crossed the street.

"They must be on they way to the store." Lil One assumed. "They gone come back through this way, watch," he concluded.

"If they do nigga, you ain't gone get no play," Crow stated.

"See why it always gotta be my nigga that be the one that hate?"

"I ain't hating. I'm just saying my nigga. You see how they actin. Them bitches probably gay."

"Naw they probably just scared because they don't know who niggas is. You gotta know how to go at 'em. Plus if they gay, I definitely want in on that." Just as Lil One had predicted, the two girls were coming back down the street with bags in their hand. Way before they got close to the car, Kiora and Bianca was crossing the street. "See, I told you they was gone come back," Lil One said.

"They phat and pretty as a bitch. Roll the window down, nigga. Watch this."

Crow rolled the window down as he was requested. As he did, Lil One honked the horn again. This time twice.

"I bet a hundred you don't get 'em to come over here."

"Aye!" Lil One yelled as he leaned over Crow, ignoring his words for the moment. "Bet that," he said. "Aye, excuse me! Let me holla at you for a minute." Lil One yelled out the window.

"Boy, what?" Kiora shouted with a fake attitude. "I'on even know you."

"Come here, you about to find out." Lil One shot back. Kiora and Bianca stopped as if they were debating whether or not they wanted to go over or not.

"They calling us over there now," Kiora said talking to BM.

"Y'all know what to do," BM told her.

Kiora and Bianca walked over to the car that Lil One and Crow sat in. Kiora pulled on Bianca as if she was forcing her to come along. Just playing her role. "Where y'all nigga from?" Kiora asked. "I ain't never seen y'all out here before."

"That don't even matter," Lil One said. "I'm tryna see where we can go."

"Wherever you tryna take me," Kiora said. " This is my friend, B." She directed the comment towards Crow.

"What's up?" Crow asked Bianca. "What you shy or some?" He questioned.

As Kiora and Bianca kept Lil One and Crow occupied, BM crept up on the passenger side of the occupied vehicle. He pulled the trigger twice placing two to Lil One's torso. The passenger's side window shattered breaking into little pieces. Kiora and Bianca ran off with a mouthful of screams. "I wish the fuck you would, lil nigga." Crow was making a reach for his pistol before BM paused his movements. "What the fuck y'all niggas watching me for?"

"Nigga wasn't nobody watching yo' ass. Nigga tryna get some pussy wit yo' cock blocking ass," Crow spazzed in response. He was highly devastated that his friend for the last ten years of his young life was gone. He was waiting for the first chance he got to grip his pistol. If he ever got one.

"Ugghh..." Lil One moaned out indicating that he was still alive. BM took his eyes off Crow for a quick second. Next thing he knew, police sirens were heard erupting close by. BM then, looked beyond the car to see if the lights were visible. Within those few seconds, Crow was able to rip the Glock from his waist. By the time he was able to lift it about to point it towards BM, he was back on point.

Bocca! Bocca! Bocca!

BM placed three into Crow's face. It was sure to be a closed casket for him.

Bocca! Bocca!

BM sent two extra random shots into Lil One, running off before the sirens rounded the corner to Mosby Street. He hurried through the cut getting away from the scene on feet.

Where Mosby Street turned into Mechanicsville Turnpike, Shy sat at the top of the hill. He watched from a distance as the whole situation played out. From his position there wasn't too much that he could do to stop what happened. Though it was something he could do to proceed.

LESSON 1.17
Prove Your Worth

The first few days of Keem's task went as normal. He got the work to his normal customers and got it gone. Soon, he found out exactly what the unknown challenge was. It was a drought throughout the city. It would make sense now that he thought about it with Mac going on vacation and all. He figured that Mac and whoever his circle is were the suppliers for the entire city. It made him realize that he wasn't too far away from the top of the food chain. Knowing that pushed his hustle to another level, he slowed down and came with a different approach. The first thing he did after pausing the movement of the work, was hiked the prices up. It was only right.

Killing two birds with one stone, Keem kept his word and reached out to an associate of that he knew from Jackson Ward. His name was Ball. Keem hit him up and placed a deal on the table for him. Ball wasn't too happy about the price but was grateful to get his hands on some work during these drying times. From there, word got out that Keem was the man to see. A lot of niggas didn't like that. Most were still trying to bounce back from that Christmas shopping and New Years partying. So, their money wasn't where it needed to be to afford Keem's numbers. Shit didn't bother him none. His team was eating, and he only dealt with the elites. The niggas that wasn't playing with the hustle but slaying it.

Meanwhile, Shy was out scheming his own plot. He held onto the burner phone though he never traveled with it. He didn't want it to be traced back to him. Instead, he communicated with Keem through his own phone. There wasn't really any big talks. All small shit. Keem just wanted to make sure that Shy kept watch on the little ones. Shy told little white lies for the next two weeks that may seem big to Keem. But later the reason would be justified.

What Shy found out was that BM was on a major come up. After he had put a hurting on Lil One, who was laid up in the hospital, and finished Crow for good, he placed the rest of his focus strictly to his hustle. For days on end, he wouldn't move. It seemed as if he didn't eat, sleep, or shit. He dedicated his entire existence to getting money. Shy had to give the nigga his props. BM was not fucking around.

After a week, it seemed like the traffic was slowing down. And then it was evident that a drought had dried up the streets. Shy was surprised when even that didn't stop BM. He thought quick on his feet and switched up hustles fast. Putting the pack down for about a good two days, BM went out on a robbing spree. Any and everybody that was worth it felt the pressure. BM took all the drugs and money that was at his disposal. Shy even watched as he finessed his way through a couple trap spots and cleaned them out. By himself. He was a one-man army. An unstoppable force. Not only did he have money stacked up of his own, but he was snatching everyone else's as well. He was also practically the only one in the hood with drugs. Afterwards, he was back to his regular grind.

As a few more days went by, slowly and surely, BM was adding a few members to his hustle forming team. He was up to something greater than Shy could see from just sitting back and watching. But Shy knew that if he remained steady long enough he would be there to see it all unfold. What he concluded was that BM was preparing for a war that he knew was on the way. He was using the youngins to post them up at the boarders of the spot he hustled at. He gave them a small pack of different drugs and made them think that they were hustlers. BM knew that they looked up to him for gun slinging legacy and that they wanted to be just like him. With knowing that, he knew that they would attempt to kill anything that tried to threaten the team's turf.

A couple times, the victims of BM's robberies tried to come through looking for revenge. Unaware of BM schemes, the first attempt was a failed one. Shots were fired before the intruders could even know what hit them. No one was hit, but the message was sent. The second time they came more prepared. BM was way ahead of the game. He pumped the youngins head up, getting them ready for the next wave of war. That one got deadly. Four got hit total and half of that total lost their lives. In the last week that was three dead, three shot, in a number of three shootouts.

Days passed and the hustle continued. For the first time though, BM actually made a move out of the Mosby Court Projects. He rented a car from a fiend. The trip surprised Shy making him second guess how clever BM really was. Shy followed him to Creighton Road where the last of the demolishing projects stood. BM stayed in the car and waited for an individual to come out of the apartment. The guy hopped in the car and the two had a short conversation. As soon as the conversation was over, BM made his way back to his neck of the woods. Shy had no idea what was about to go down, but he knew it was something big and unexpected.

As Shy tailed BM back to Mosby Court, he thought he was tripping. After double checking the rearview though, he knew that was far from the truth. He was being followed as well. He made a left turning into Lucky's store parking lot. What he found out was that the car wasn't following him. They were actually following BM. He lead them up the hill to the top of Mosby. Shy jumped back into traffic hurrying to get back on track. The two cars drove themselves into the apartments all the way at the very top of Mosby Court

Projects. Shy knowing that the apartments were one way in and one way out, made the wise decision not to follow the train into the gates of the apartments.

Shy sat as close as he could to them. He wanted to wait and see how long the cars would stay up the hill. He didn't have to wait long to find out. Within three minutes, so many shots rang out into the air you could have mistaken it for a college drumming band. The exchange in the gunfire went on for a good two minutes. To Shy, it seemed like ten. Seconds later, both cars sped down the hill zooming right pass Shy as they made their escape. "Thats a slimy ma'fucka." Shy admitted to himself. "Damn."

***

"Aye, they say it's going down right now out Mosby," D-Roc announced after hanging up the phone. He made his way over to E who was sitting at the table. He was deep into a chess game with his cellie. "They say niggas just went up there two cars deep and shot the place up."

"Shit probably wasn't nobody but Maine and them. You know they beefing hard wit Tez and them right now." E assumed without even looking up from the chess board.

"Naw brah. The hood already saying it wasn't Maine or Tez."

"How the hell they gone know that? You said it was just happening right?"

"Yeah, a few minutes ago. That was my brotha I was just on the phone with. He say Maine and Tez calling errbody phone around Mosby tryna see who the hell did I.?" D-Roc and E had come to a mutual understanding after getting into their fight. They even conversed topics bringing them a little closer together. Plus, it didn't hurt that they were the only two Mosby niggas on the tier with what they would usually call the opps.

"Oh yeah?" E was sounding a little more interested in the conversation now. "Anybody died off that shit?"

They say niggas from both sides died from that shit. And whoever it was went at both spots. I'on know the numbers. I just know that five niggas got hit out that bitch. And on top of that, they say yo' boy, BM been going crazy out that bitch lately. Say he got the whole bottom of Mosby on lock and he getting money out that ma'fucka too. Say that nigga went on a robbing spree for like two or three days. Jackin' the whole hood. Niggas tried to get back at his ass, but he was on point."

"Yeah, I heard most of that shit already," E stated only telling half of the truth. Honestly, he heard a lot more than that. But he decided to keep it to himself. He didn't want anybody to know about his ill will towards BM. The best way for him to do that was to talk about him as less as possible. So with that, he changed the subject. "You think them Ward or Creighton niggas had some to do with that shit though?"

"Shidd... I'on know who could be behind that shit. Mosby beefin' with so many people," D-Roc said taking a seat on top of the table next to E. "For real though. The way niggas say they rushed the spot, it was an inside type shit. Like it was definitely a Mosby nigga. I'on know though."

"Aye Taz, Pound!" E called out to the tier.

"Brah, don't do no dumb shit," D-Roc said a little concerned. But not too much. "It's only two of us on this tier fool."

"Yoo!" Taz yelled back.

"Naw, I ain't on shit," E responded to D-Roc. "I wouldn't even put you in that position," he said with assurance. "Aye y'all niggas pull up right quick."

"What's good?" Pound skipped his way towards E with a bob. Taz was on the way as well.

"Niggas jus hit Mosby hard," E said carelessly. "Y'all heard anything about that joint?"

"Naw, I did just get off the phone with the gurl. Shawty say it went crazy out that bitch," Taz spoke. "But the jects ain't have none to do with that joint, if that's what you asking."

"Yeah, if it was us we would have been on point about that." Pound assisted. "For real brah and they tryna to see who was on that mission themselves. Say niggas did that. No cap brah." Pound tried to say as respectfully as possible.

"Yeah, I'm tryna see myself," E said. "I'm about to get on the line and see wat I can code up."

"You think it was them Creighton niggas?" Taz guessed.

"I doubt it." E guessed himself. "You never know though. Go see if you can get word from one of them niggas."

"Them niggas don't fuck with me," Taz said. "Go holla at em, Pound." He looked towards his homeboy. "You do one always playing cards and shit with them niggas."

"Yeah," Pound agreed. "For special moments like dis. Wing team nigga." He patted underneath his arm right below his arm pit twice then walked headed off to his mission.

"Checkmate," E's cellie humbly said.

E gave him a fist pound. "Let me get on this horn right quick," he said as he was getting up from the table. "I'll be right back."

E spent exactly thirty minutes on the phone. All he found out was that the hood was in total chaos. It was crawling with police like roaches in a project kitchen at two o'clock in the morning.

E sat in the chair at the phone for a minute trying to figure out who was brave enough and smart enough to pull a move like that off. Usually, he was always able to get his ears so close to the street that he could hear the tires rolling over it. In the back of his mind, he was hurt that he couldn't hit up his main source. Then, it hit him, BM. He been trying to keep that nigga off his mind so much that he never even expected him. But then again, on second thought, he counted BM out. He was a force to be playing with true indeed. But he was too selfish and greedy to have the ability to put a team together that was that strong. Or so he thought.

C.O. Crawford walked on the tier and everything E thought about had vanished like a magic trick. He hopped up and met her at the C.O's desk. "You ain't bring me none to eat?" Was the first thing he said knowing that she was coming back from her late lunch break.

"No, boy. You know I can't do that," Crawford replied wishing that she could. Over these last two weeks, E had grew on her fast. He had healed up, only adding to his sex appeal and she was able to witness the respect, power, and control that he had. She loved the way he moved in a room full of vultures. He moved alone, standing solid at all times. She even tried him out a couple times by telling him a few things about herself. Just to see if it would come back to her. He never spoke a word about what they spoke about.

"Come on, Crawford. A nigga hungry. You know I'm tryna eat." E played as if he was really starving, rubbing on his stomach.

"Boy yo' ass ain't hungry! All them swoles and all that stuff you be making. You got a cell full of food. Matter of fact, you need to start making me something to eat so I can save some money. Shit, I like wraps, cassadas, and stuff like that. Oodle Noodles and shit." Crawford laughed her own comment off playfully. E loved it when she laughed.

"That's what I'm sayin'. If you feed me, you gone eat too. The plate gone be so full that saving is gone be yo' least worry. That shit gone come in so fast, it's gone pile up like snow in a blizzard." E's expression on his face was dead serious. The way Crawford looked at him told him that she understood what he was saying. This wasn't the first time he mentioned the idea to her. Usually, she'd shut the topic off. But being that she never wrote him a charge or told on him, let him know that she would take the bait one day. All he needed was a way to get her hooked on.

"You must really think you can do some shit like that and get away with it?" She asked really just saying, as if it was unheard of. "You tryna make me lose my job or something? I thought you liked seein' me?" She was still playing.

"First of all, you have to take this shit serious. Cuz all that playing might leave a lil room for era. And no, we can't afford that. Second, you right. I'm not gone be able to do this by myself. Neither would you. Together though... unstoppable."

"You really serious about this, ain't you?"

"As serious as fighting a life sentence."

"Okay, so let's just say, hypothetically right?"

"Uh-huh." E was anxious for her to continue.

"I... well we, decided to do some. How you think we would be able to make it?" She was curious. It was the question she had been dying to ask. E knew then that he had her.

"I'ma keep it real. I'll start you off slow. Let you test drive the whip so you can get a feel of it. But I promise you we could make no less than a band in a week and that's just giving cushion." Crawford had an unimpressed look on her face.

"But when we really get to rolling, like highway speed, we lookin at bout ten to fifteen bands a month. And that's stayin' under the radar money. We can push twenty but none over that because I rather keep you safe first."

Crawford could sense the seriousness and genuineness in his voice. She even seen it in his eyes. Her intuition told her that he was the one. Everything that she had manifested in the past was coming to the present. "Okay," she said. E's heart jumped for joy like a man who had just hit a billion-dollar lottery. "We gone hold off on this right quick. Take this round with me. Let's throw it off with some mediocre talk. Then when we get back you can let me know what it is that I exactly need to do."

"Aight bet." E agreed happily but humble.

"I'm telling you now though, if it's some crazy shit, I'm not doin' it." She was dead ass serious. Even pointed her finger in his face.

"Trust me shawty, this shit gone be as easy as counting to three." They walked around the tier as planned. Everybody on the tier knew that E was up to something with C.O. Crawford. It wasn't hard to see that she had chosen him. Out of respect, most niggas stayed out of the way of E's work. Truthfully, a lot of them was rooting for him to get her. Some even so while hating at the same time. At the end, they all wanted the same thing and that was for that sack to hit. There were still a couple clowns that intervened every now and then blindly and knowingly. E never tripped though. He knew his worth, and so did she.

***

Keem walked through the front door of Club Jungle with a bag on his back and one in each hand. Mac sat at the bar with Chop and Blade. "Keem, nice of you to join us." Mac invited. "We were just conversing about you."

"Yeah, spoke the devil right on up," Chop said. Blade laughed.

"Hope it was all good," Keem said talking mainly to Mac, ignoring his two large pawns. "Shidd... about the devil?" Chop asked with a coughing chuckle. "Hell naw.." Blade joined in with a laugh again. Keem dropped the two bags that was in his hands at Mac's feet and handed him the one off his back.

"I'ma need this bag back. It's my personal favorite. It's all there though. I even through in a lil extra. You know, an act of gratitude," Keem said with pride dusting the invisible dirt off his shoulders.

"Told you," Chop said to Blade in their side conversation. "Give me my money. I knew he had it in 'em. Got it from his pops."

"I never doubted you one second, Keem," Mac said. "And you know what? I'm glad I was right."

"Told you," Keem said. "I'm playing for keeps."

"I can see that. Glad you're on my team. Take a seat, have a drink." Mac offered. "This calls fo a celebration."

"How 'bout we take a rain check?" Keem advised. "Tonight maybe? I gotta go handle some real important right now."

"Okay. Thats cool. Handle yo' business. I respect that about you. Work first then play later."

"Bet." Keem made his way back out of the club and hopped back in his ride. "Aye Siri, call Shy."

"Yo," Shy answered, his voice blaring through the car speakers connected to the Bluetooth.

"What's up? You good? Why you blowing my shit up like that?"

"Naw, I need to see you. Like now."

"Where?"

"You know."

"On my way."

"Say no more."

Keem pulled up round Hillside to meet up with Shy. His little brother climbed into his car and gave him the run down on BM for the last two weeks. He even had to inform him about Crow's death and Lil One being shot. Keem had passed one task with flying colors but failed the other drastically. He was so focus on upping his hustle that he had forgotten all about them little niggas altogether. I mean, it crossed his mind once or twice, but the grind always required his full attention. Hell, he hadn't even talked to his own brother while he was on his run. Most phone conversations were cut completely.

Surprisingly, but not really. Shy was already on it. "Brah that nigga BM on some other shit! He taking slimy to the next level." Shy sounded a little crazed with his expression, but Keem still heard him out. "This nigga opened the back door on his own hood. He shot up the place with a bunch of Creighton niggas!"

"What?" Keem asked unbelievable.

"Exactly. And a few days before that, he robbed damn near the whole hood. It looked like a drought had come through or some." That part Keem knew was for sure to be true. Still, he remained quiet. "Cuz after that it was like BM was one of the only niggas round there with shit to sell. Niggas try to get back, but by that time he convinced a few lil niggas to lock in wit 'em. And he set Crow and Lil One up good. I saw the whole thing. Before I realized what was happening, it was too late. I couldn't do shit about it. The nigga sent two young baddies at 'em. They trained right too and played they part to a tee. I think the nigga plotting to take over the whole Mosby for real. The nigga already got the bottom on smash!" Shy threw extra inferences on his last word expressing just how real it was.

Keem took in all Shy said. He concluded that not only was Shy extra observant, but he was also smart as hell. "So, you was able to see all of this the whole time without being noticed?"

"Yep," Shy replied as if it was nothing. Truth is Shy had saved Keem in more ways than he knew it. After all, this was his plug's son that they were discussing. Keem counted ten bands from his pockets. He gave it to Shy. "What's dis for?"

"Stay on that nigga," Keem ordered.

"Gotcha." Shy was already about to get out of the car.

"Aye." Keem stopped him. "Change yo' whip up and be careful."

"I thought you was about to tell me some I ain't know. Love you fool."

"Love you more nigga."

LESSON 1.18
Never Get Too Comfortable

Taking Shawndra's instruction, Derek used the number to call her. What he found was a disturbing conformation. Shawndra had told him all that he had expected was true. She even presented the proofs of her truths. With that, she convinced Derek to help set her plan into action.

After taking a few days to make sure that everyone was on the same page, now was the time to go. Derek had falsely reductively allowed Kimberly to use the car. But not before attaching a tracking device on it. Kimberly was so accustomed to his routine that even her conscious was confused to the wrongs that she committed. She was so concentrated on her conceit that she never saw it coming.

Shawndra grabbed Kimberly by the weave and slammed her head against the window. As Kimberly's body fell to the ground, Shawndra released her grip on the tracks. "I'ma teach you 'bout fucking with another bitch's man!" Shawndra gave Kimberly a powerful and painful kick to the stomach. It took no time for Kimberly to join in. Together, they put four feet all over the body of Kimberly.

"Aight... Shawn," Kadesha said putting a stop to their whooping. "You had enough yet hoe?" She snapped at the defenseless victim.

"Uugghh..." Was all Kimberly could say expressing her pain.

"Come on girl, let's get dis bitch up," Kimberly stated to Shawndra. Together, they helped Kimberly who was so scared for her life that wouldn't dare to look the two in their faces. "Call that nigga up and tell his ass to come out cha hoe. Tell his ass you gotta a lil surprise for 'em."

"Uh?" Kimberly acted as if she was blind to her situation. As if she was innocent to the karma that she attracted.

Kimberly jumped out of shock when she heard the sound of a cocking pistol. Shawndra had pulled a M & P .22 from under her pants. She quickly placed the pistol underneath Kimberly's chin with extreme force. "Bitch you keep playing with me and I'ma blow yo' fuckin tongue out yo' mouth."

Kimberly started to cry. "Hold up, Shawn." Kadesha interrupted. "Bitch shut up yo' hoe ass up!" She directed her attention back towards Kimberly. "And stop acting like you don't know what fuck going on. Now, call that nigga out cha or we gone replace yo' life with his. And make it sound sexy. You know how to play it hoe."

"Okay. Okay, can I get my phone?" Shawndra took Kimberly's phone out for him to answer. He did so on the first ring. "Naw, I am outside. Cuz I want to take you out somewhere. It's a special surprise. Well, put some clothes on then boy! And hurry up!" She hung the phone up. "He said he coming in five minutes."

Shawndra and Kadesha went to post in the cut on the back of 25th Street dragging Kimberly along with them. They waited around the corner for Tank to come out the back door of the apartment. He swaggered out dripping sauce as he walked. He looked to the right up the cut of his pocket, he doubled tapped the screen bringing it to life.

"Stop moving you son of a bitch bastard." Tank looked up at the sudden sound of Shawndra's voice. She stood about six feet away from him holding the firearm up towards his face. "You better not take another fuckin step." Shawndra's face was covered with painful hate.

"Shawndra, what the fuck is you doing?" Tank's face expressed puzzlement.

"Don't act like you don't know, nigga!" Shawndra's voice squeaked from the pain that pumped from her heart. "All these fuckin years. I'd hoped that you would one day man up. But you ain't no man. You's a fuckin animal, a damn dog."

"Look Shawndra, whatever it is that's got you so upset, I'll make it up to you."

Tank snuck a step forward. Shawndra took one backwards. As she did, the grip on the gun tightened. Tank noticed her eagerness and froze. He didn't want to force her to apply the seven pounds to the trigger causing it to explode. "Shawndra, please just think 'bout what you doin'." Tank was so anxious to get his hands on Shawndra's gun that he hadn't even noticed that he had taken another step. It was definitely a wrong move.

Shawndra couldn't think fast enough to stop herself. The emotions of her hurt and pain sent her energy in motion. She squeezed the trigger three times. All three shots were placed to Tank's torso. He was unexpectedly surprised. But instead of going to the corner of the building she was behind and sent a bullet flying to Tank's skull. His body had instantly flopped to the ground.

Pac! Pac!

Kadesha shot him twice more for death assurance.

Shawndra had frozen after she shot Tank. If it wasn't for Kadesha, Tank probably would've made it to Shawndra. Kimberly had screamed in fear. It annoyed the shit out Kadesha to the point it was hard to hear herself think. With lack of hesitation, she fearlessly took Kimberly's life by shooting her directly in her temple. Just like that, Kimberly's voice was silenced forever.

LESSON 1.19
Keep What You Know to Yourself

Roxy busted into her brother room unannounced without an invite.

"P!" She basically shouted after damn near slamming the door up against the wall. P was in the midst of multitasking. Counting money and breaking down pounds of weed.

"What, bitch?" P shouted back. The interruption from his sister had placed him on edge. It pissed him off even more because he lost count.

"Watch yo' mouth, nigga!" Roxy shot back.

"Whatever. What the fuck you want doe? Don't you see I'm doing something?

"Yeah," Roxy responded nonchalantly. "Let me hold two hundred dollars?" She asked while literally holding her handout.

"I ain't giving you shit. You better get the fuck out my face."

"Tight pocket ass nigga." Roxy expressed with much attitude.

"Whatever." He tried his best to ignore her. "Get out!"

"Naw for real though." Roxy turned a bit more serious as she attended to her initial purpose for bothering P. "You ain't seen or heard from Keem? I been tryna hit that nigga up. He ain't returning none of my calls though."

"Naw. He tried to hit me up a couple weeks ago, but I ain't been getting back with 'em for real. I guess he got the point and stop calling."

"What? That's probably why he ain't been answering my fuckin calls." Roxy jumped to the conclusion. "Why would you be ducking 'em anyway? That nigga spend plenty money with you and bring plenty of clientele." She slapped P in his face with the facts right after she asked him as a matter of fact like question. Still after saying all of that, she headed into the room and took a seat on P's bed.

"Shit bigger than money for real. I just had to fall back from the nigga." P took the fourteen grams of weed off the scale and placed it in the bag with the other half, making it a whole ounce. He repeated the process while remaining silent. Roxy sat in silence as well. She stared at him paying steady attention as if she was waiting for the rest of the answer. He was hesitant to continue but did so anyway. "I know Keem known as being a stand-up nigga. And I thought I could trust em."

Roxy's anxiety was overriding her patience, which caused her to become a bit frustrated trying to piece together the meaning of P's words. "We not in kindergarten, P." She shot back up to her snappy attitude. "You don't have to talk in riddles. We grown as a bitch." Roxy stopped and looked at P with impatience.

"I think that nigga Keem killed Ace." P shot it out of his mouth hoping that the words would somehow go over Roxy's head.

"Wait," Roxy was now confused. "What you mean? That's that boy's best friend. Why would you think that?"

"I know the shit sound crazy. But that night we went to the club on New Years Eve, both of them niggas had went missing. I ain't pay that shit too much of mind for real. But like a good few days after that, niggas was lookin for Ace, like he was missing or something. Keem said some bout Ace going down to Miami the last he knew."

"So, why would you assume about something you don't have proof of?" Roxy sounded as if she was defending Keem, assuming that P's assumption was wrong.

"I'm just making sure I watch who I got round me," P said in self-defense. "Cuz, say I was right. I'on wanna be the next nigga he clipped for whatever reason."

"I see what you saying but I'on think he would do no shit like that to Ace. If it wasn't no nigga he loved out there, I know he loves Ace."

"You don't know who that man loves."

"Whatever." Roxy stood up and headed towards the door.

"And don't go running yo' mouth either, bitch."

"Fuck you, pussy. You probably run yo mouth more than I do." Right before she stepped through the door seal, Roxy patted her right hand on her right ass cheek. "Kiss my ass." She went straight in her room and closed the door. She laid across her bed and reached for her phone. She went into her message to send Keem a text. Before doing so, she saw that her last six messages were still not responded and unread as well.

Keem 'HMU ASAP. It's important. I heard some bout U and Ace. Jus wanna PYOG'.

Lately Roxy's pockets had been dry, and her pussy has been wet. She could have easily gotten a few drips of cum from a multiple selection of niggas. But her thirst was for Keem. For her own selfish desires, she would use the little bit of information that P had just ran past her for bait. Keem was a big fish. Roxy just hoped that he would bight.

***

"Damn bitch, you gone suck all the THC out the gas," Pike spoke to his girlfriend Markisha as they shared a blunt together. While in the middle of the smoke session, the two were also in the middle of a conversation.

"Boy, fuck you." Markisha sent the blunt back over to Pike. Now why you say you think BM shot E? And why you think he got some to do with that store robbery and with Ron and Ike getting killed?"

"Cuz word on the street was that two niggas in that robbery got away and that one had got hit in the shoulder. That day BM had scored from me, the nigga was holding his shoulder funny. Like the shit was stiff or something. I wanted to ask 'em what was up with him. I minded my business though. Shit just didn't make sense though.

"All of a sudden, BM came up big, E get shot and BM actin like he green to the shit. Like him and E ain't in errthing together. The drought hit, everybody get robbed and then niggas shoot up the APTs."

"And you think BM behind all dis shit that's going on?"

"I know his ass is. I'm telling you," Pike said with great assurance.

"I ain't never trust that nigga anyway," Markisha stated. "Thats why I haven't been over Tisha's house lately, cuz his ass always over there now."

Pike got a call through his cell phone. "Gotta play right quick. I'll be back," he said after hanging up the phone. He placed a kiss on Markisha's lips and headed towards the door.

"Be careful, Pike!" She shouted to his back as he traveled down the hallway.

"I stay strapped!" Pike shouted without looking back.

Markisha waited until she heard the apartment door close followed by the screen door slamming before she picked up her phone. She found the contact she searched for and dialed the number.

"Hello," she heard the woman on the other end of the phone answer.

"Tisha," Markisha stated making sure it her. Although she knew it was.

"Yeah, gurl. Who else?" Tisha asked nonchalantly.

"Can you talk?" Tisha knew that was code that what she was about to hear was for her ears only.

"Yeah. You good. What's up?" Tisha was in the middle of a nap before the call had interrupted it. Now the boiling tea had her waking up alert.

"You need to be careful around that baby maniac."

Tisha chuckled lightly. "Girl, tell me some that I don't fuckin know. What's wrong though? Cuz you said that as if the whole fuckin' Mosby don't know that already. It had to be another reason."

"Well, I know you heard that E got shot New Years Eve?"

"Uh huh."

"Well, I just got word that BM was the one that shot him."

"What?"

"And he was in on that robbery with Ron and Ike. That's the reason he shot E. He must've robbed E for the money that they got out the store."

"Where you—"

"How you think he getting all that money?"

"He ain't—"

"I mean I ain't gone say that he was a broke nigga before, but bitch the nigga is in his bag deeper than ever before." Markisha barely allowed Tisha to get a word in. On top of that, she spoke as if she was certainly sure of what she was saying.

Tisha and Markisha were sisters. Twins at that. They were closer than the usual siblings. Lately though, ever since BM's invasion of Tisha's apartment, Markisha stayed far away from her residence. Markisha never liked to be in the presence of BM from the jump. Now, she felt for the protection of her sister.

"Okay. Okay! Marki, I hear you girl damn." Tisha was finally able to say. "But what do you want me to do about all that?"

"I'on know sis," Markisha answered honestly. "Just watch that nigga. Be careful and don't get caught up in none of his bullshit, please."

"Gurl you know I'on do none but lay up in dis house, wait for my son to get out school and mind my business." Tisha released a sigh. "Thank you for putting me on game though. And don't trip, I'ma make sure I keep that nigga in line when it comes down to me and Lil' Slay's safety."

"Aight sis. I love you. I just wanted to make sure you was aware of the shit that nigga was in. Call me if you need me."

"Aight gurl. I love you more."

"And Tisha," Markisha shouted through the phone before the call was disconnected. "You ain't hear none of that shit from me."

"I already know, sis." The call was ended. "BM!" Then Tisha called out from upstairs in her bedroom. "BM! Bring yo' ass here now!"

A few seconds later, BM was bolting up the steps full of energy. "Yo! What's up?" His face was puzzled. "Why the hell you yellin' like you ready kill something?"

"Why the fuck people saying that you shot E?" Tisha came straight out.

"Who the fuck is people?" BM did his best at playing the question off. Truth was though that the question caught him off guard like a sucker punch. "And why would you even believe some dumb ass shit like that?" This wasn't the first time that BM had heard this. They were definitely surfacing. But this was the first time that he was approached about the topic.

"I don't believe it, first of all. And I hope I'm right." If there wasn't anybody that knew about the love that E had for BM, it would be Tisha. She saw it firsthand. "And it don't matter who saying it, just know that people are saying it and it got to me. Therefore, I brought it to you because I wanted to know. I mean I think I at least deserve that much since you turned my kitchen into yo' trap spot. All types of killings and shootings been popping up close to my apartment and shit. We won't be having all that shit near this building before yo' ass got back down here. All that shit takes place down the street or up the hill in the top of Mosby."

BM could hear the annoyance in Tisha's voice and sighted the worry on her face. "Look you ain't got none to worry about. You out of all people should know that I would never do anything to hurt E." BM lied with a straight face using their past history to fabricate the truth. "I appreciate you keeping it real and bringing what you heard to me. But that shit some straight bullshit." BM wasn't slow by a long shot. He knew that it was only a couple people who Tisha communicated with. Cutting out the other option, he went straight to the assumption of Markisha, Tisha's sister. He thought back on the conversation that he had with Pike. Placing two and two together, he figured that Pike must have been pillow talking to Markisha and that's how his situation came up.

"You know I've always had yo' back BM, through thick and thin. Just don't have a bitch out here in the blind and shit. How the fuck I'm supposed to watch out for you if you taking a bitch sight away?" Tisha was sincere and her question was a legitimate one. No matter how real Tisha kept it with him, BM just couldn't bring himself to trust her at all. After almost six years, he was still salty about her choosing Slay over him. He was reminded every time he looked at Lil Slay. It hurt his pride and set his ego on fire.

"Like I said Ti," BM leaned in close enough to Tisha's face to plant a light kiss to her cheek. "You don't have none to worry about." Standing up, he made his exit out of room without saying another word.

BM headed back to the back porch to his past. What a coincidence it was for him to see Pike coming around the corner of the building. "Aye Pike, what's up my nigga?" BM asked approaching with false happiness.

"BM, what's good my nigga?" Pike played his part as well. "What, you ready for the re-up already?"

"Hell naw, fool. Not right now. I'll definitely be ready for you by tonight though." Pike approached and BM stuck his hand out for a dap. They embraced due to mutual respect. "What's up though? You ain't heard none 'bout E situation lately? It seems like the streets sweeping that shit under the rug and I ain't to much feeling that shit." BM was really checking Pike's temperature. Looking for any signs of negative body language, fake confused facial expressions, or even a defensive tone of voice.

Pike released a sigh before shocking the hell out of BM. "I'ma keep it real wit you, fool," he stated. "It ain't lookin good for the home team."

"What you mean? Get to the point."

"Point blank period. Niggas is saying that you was the mastermind behind that shit. Matter of fact, word is that yo' name been on errthing that's been popping out dis bitch. They even think it was you who shot the APTs up. Ma'fuckin Tez and Maine out cha putting they sources together tryna figure out who was behind it. Shit is all pointing back to you, my nigga."

BM was at a loss for words. Of course, he knew all the speculations he was hearing was true. But the fact that Pike kept it so gangster silenced him. "Only thing I can say my nigga," Pike continued, "is thank you for sparing me, nigga, for real."

LESSON 1.20
The Past Catches Up

Keem stumbled into his baby mother's house at exactly three thirty-three in the morning. Worried to death, she sat there in the dark awaiting his arrival. He never noticed that she was ever there, until "Keem," she said.

"What the fuck?" The sudden startle sobered him up some. "What type of shit you on?" He flicked on the light removing the darkness from the room.

"I've been blowin' yo' phone up all night." She was calm, which was scary.

"I told you I was going out with Mac tonight. Remember? I even asked you did you want to go." He saw the missed calls but missed them on purpose.

"Yeah, I do remember. And no, I did not want to go. But when I call yo' phone, especially that many times, I expect you to answer. Or at least, call me back." Her voice was stern and deeply demanding.

"Yeah, you right." Keem knew he was wrong. So, there was no need to argue. "But you up in here like somebody done died or some."

"I hope not," she said unsure.

"What you mean?" Keem, growing confused, took a seat beside her. "What's wrong? You okay though?"

"I haven't seen or heard from my brother in about two weeks now." Her voice had begun to crack as her eyes welled

155

up with tears. "He ain't answering the phone or none. And you wasn't answering yours either. It started to scare me."

Keem wrapped an arm around Monique and pulled her in close. She buried her face into his chest. "I'll hit the streets and see if I find some out. His ass probably found him a lil broad to duck off wit or something. I'm sure it ain't no crazy shit. But I'll find out for you." Keem kissed the top of her forehead. He was glad that she was unable to see his face. That way she wouldn't be able to see the lies in his eyes.

"I swear I hope you're right." She placed her faith into Keem's words.

The next afternoon, Keem was up and out the house. He couldn't wait to get out of there. As soon as he hopped in the car, his phone started to ring. He noticed the number and answered the call. "Yo."

"Aye!" It was Deuce. He was Ace's little brother. "You ain't seen my brother?" His voice was aggressively packed with determination.

"What you mean, have I seen him?" Keem answered a question with a question. That was the first sign of guilt. Sitting in the Range, he roamed his eyes while taking note of his surroundings. "I thought he was with you." Keem covered his guilt with falsehood.

"I'on know what makes you say that. When the word is that the last time he was seen was with you. At Club Jungle. New Years Eve."

Keem knew that this day would come. He was surprised that it took this long. Out of all the things he was able to prepare for, this was one of the hardest. "Yeah, we turned up and after that he said he was posed to meet up with you." Keem sat behind the steering wheel shifting his eyes from mirror to mirror. "He said y'all niggas was posed to take a trip down Miami for a week or so. On some vacation shit."

"Yeah, we was. But he never showed up. And you say he told you this?"

"Yeah nigga," Keem lied with confidence. "That nigga even asked me if I wanted to go with y'all. Why, what's wrong though? You telling me some happened to my nigga or some?"

"Mane, I ain't heard from my brother since the morning of New Years Eve. At first, I ain't really trip too much. I just chalked it up as his normal routine. Then, errbody else start hitting my phone looking for his ass."

"Aight look, I'ma do some homework. Check on a few of his on the low hoes. See if the nigga hiding out ducked off or something. You know the streets been on fire and a drought came through. So, he might just be out the way somewhere for real. Don't trip. I'm on this shit."

"Aye, Keem,"

"What's good, fool?"

"If some happened to my brother mane—"

"If some happened to yo' brother, I'ma make the whole city pay for the shit. Nigga the funeral home gone have a heavy flow of income." In a way, Keem's words were true. Only if he hadn't been the murderer himself.

"Aight bet. Say no more." Deuce hung the phone up.

Trying to keep the streets from blowing up his temper, Keem leaned his headrest of the seat. "Now I gotta blow some fake smoke behind this disloyal ass nigga." He went through his phone checking for notifications. All was normal, except a text that stuck out to him. It was from Roxy. After reading the text, he shook his head. "Fuck!" He immediately thought of P. That was the only logical explanation. He sat for a couple more minutes trying to clear his mind.

The pyramid scheme was tricky. The higher you climbed in an attempt to get closer to the cap stone, the slimmer your wiggle room became to maneuver. Even though he was heading up the ladder of success, it seemed that the walls were closing in on him the more he ascended. Pressure from the water that busted pipes, apply that same pressure to coal and you'll make a diamond. Keem was definitely feeling the pressure that came with success. Since he never was the type to fold under pressure, he had to find a way to transform it into treasure.

He wasn't quite sure how he would piece together his triumph. But with the right idea he knew it would come into formation nicely. This what he was good at. Strategy was the same thing that got him where he was now. It was definitely too late to cry now. Ace was gone. Mo was gone. And neither were coming back. Ever.

LESSON 1.21
Tying Up Loose Ends

Keem rolled off the exit of the highway, getting on Washington street. As he cruised through the city of Petersburg, he thought of the regret that he had in his mind. For some reason unknown to him, he was already feeling like coming to Peterburg was a bad decision. He tried to convince his intuition that it was something that needed to be done. He wanted to holler at Roxy face to face. Nothing over the phone. The topic was too serious. Although he doubted what truth Roxy really knew, his curiosity still ate at his brain.

He pulled up in front of Roxy's crib and hopped out. Peeking at the phone for the time which read 1:21 AM, he had no plans of being in there no longer than five minutes. Therefore, he made a mental deadline to be out by 1:26AM.

Roxy already excitedly awaited Keem's arrival was anxiously waiting at the door for him.

"Hey Keem," she expressed gleefully. Hastily taking steps towards Keem with open arms, she wrapped them around Keem's neck and tried to pull her in closer. Keem applied a light touch to his hug before using his hand to peel Roxy off his body. Once he did, she stood on her tippy toes with her lips poked out in search for a kiss. Keem turned his head and brushed pass her crossing the entrance to the door seal.

"What's the matter with you?" She questioned as she tugged at the tail to the backend of his shirt. Roxy followed him and closed the door behind herself. "You don't miss me?" The way her voice sounded you would've thought she was a five year old asking for some candy that she was denied.

"So, what's up with dis shit you texted me?" Keem asked getting straight to the business. "I ain't got long."

"Huh? What?" Roxy asked completely confused. She had in her mind that Keem was there to satisfy her sexual appetite. "You don't want none of mommy's cookie?"

"Naw, a nigga ain't got time for all that right now."

Roxy's flopped down on the couch disappointed with a sudden pout upon her face.

Keem remained standing. "I got some other shit I gotta handle in a few minutes."

"So, what you come all the way down here for? I could've just told what you needed to know on the phone."

"Cuz, this type of shit don't need to be talked about over the phone." Keem was speeding and getting impatient. "Naw come on." Put me on game. So, I can go."

"I ain't telling you shit." Roxy called his bluff. "You want the word on the streets and I want some dick. You know how it go, nigga. Game ain't free."

As fast as a shooting star, Keem thrust his hand towards Roxy's neck, wrapping them around her throat. He squeezed with the strength of a crazed man, choking her to the point of gagging.

"Listen here bitch!" His voice was angry. Roxy never ever had witnessed this side of Keem. She had only heard stories of his short-fused attitude. The only type of aggression she ever witnessed from him was sexual. I guess that's what lead her to think that she was expecting from becoming a victim. She definitely wished she had folded now. "I'on know who the fuck you got me fucked up with.

But I ain't that nigga to be fucking playing with! Do you fuckin hear me? Huh bitch?"

Of course, Roxy couldn't verbally respond. Instead, she nodded as best as she could with Keem's hands around her neck like a brace. The front opened and in P came walking in. His hands was full of McDonald's bags. His head was looking downward as he stumbled through the floor.

"Roxy I got yo' broke hungry ass some to eat." P engaged in their shit talking ritual. I dropped yo' soda when I was getting out the car though. So, your cum drinking ass gone have to go back to quench yo' thrust."

"Ugghh. Ugg." P lifted his head up at the moment he heard the choking sound.

"What the fuck y'all in dis bitch doing?" The look in both Roxy's and Keem's eyes said it all. Keem's eye's searched for murder, while Roxy's eyes saw death approaching. P's eyes widened with fear. Not for the fear of Keem's presence, though extremely surprised. Another surprising fact was that the fear was for the life of his sister. He used that fear to stand in front of it, allowing it to push him into action. Dropping the contents from his hand, P charged towards Keem with force.

Keem was in such a rage in strangling Roxy that he basically was blind to P's approach. By the time he was fully aware, P was taking him to the floor.

"Fuck off my sister, nigga." Even though P was completely blind to the gist of the situation at hand, this was one of the main reasons why he despised his sister's sexual dealings against a double-edged sword.

A freshly relieved Roxy jumped to her feet and rushed over to the two tumbling bodies on the floor. "Bitch ass nigga!" She spat on her way. "I'm the wrong bitch to fuck with!" She cocked her leg back as if she was at home plate preparing to contact an approaching rolling kick ball. With all her sexual frustration, the built up anger from the last minute or so, along with the rare demonstration of love that her brother was displaying, Roxy exploded a powerful kick to Keem's face.

"Aww! Bitch!" Keem expressed his pain. Almost immediately after Roxy was following up with a strap to his head, causing it to pound the floor of the living room. She was looking to take advantage of her revengeful opportunity. Roxy cocked her leg again. Before the kicking attempt could be made, Keem grabbed hold of her planted foot. He yanked at it causing her to lose balance. Falling backwards, her body crashed into the wooden living room table. The pain placed her body into a stagnant shock.

P drove his fist into Keem's jaw. With his back against the floor, Keem swung but missed his target. P placed a knee into Keem's chest and wrapped both hands around Keem's throat. The tables had turned swiftly as karma freed Keem of his debts. P panted as his adrenaline clouded his common sense. Each second that passed, pressed more pressure to Keem's throat. Really, he didn't want to kill Keem. Although, in the back of his mind that was the only choice he truthfully had. He had no doubt at all that Keem would most likely kill them both if he spare him.

"You know I couldn't just watch you choke my sister out and I'on do none." For some reason, P had took to explaining himself. "You know a nigga got respect for you."

Keem stretched his arm out as his eyes rolled back and forth to the back of his eyes. The little lines in them had been recolored red. He struggled for what little air he could breathe. "I expected the same shit from you nigga."

"P! Stop!" Roxy regained consciousness and was able to crawl to her hands and knees. "You gone kill him." P heard his sister's words and took a deep look into Keem's eyes. As he did, he could see life slowly leaking out of Keem's body. Keem's life was literally in P's hands. "P! Stop!"

For reason's unknown to his own understanding, P released his grip on Keem's neck. Blessed with the full abilities to breathe a breath of air again, Keem deeply inhaled. His exhalation came with a loud cough. By the time he could fully take in another breath of air, Keem's palm was wrapped around the handle of his pistol. On his second exhale, a bullet was exiting the muzzle of the gun. It flew through the wind, ironically tapping into P's lung.

Roxy screamed a fearful tone. Now, P was the one inhaling deeply in an attempt to catch his breath.

Boc! Boc! Boc!

Keem didn't even wait for P to exhale before snatching his breath away forever.

"Nooo!!" A lifetime full of regrets rushed Roxy's heart as she watched the only family member that she knew of die quickly right before her eyes. All the hate she gave her brother she wished she could replace with love. All her foul hurtful words she wished she could take back. Immediately, she finally realized exactly how much she actually loved P. It made her sick to her stomach that he had to lose his life behind her in order for her to understand.

"Ugghhh." Roxy threw up a pile of her stomach contents on the floor. Only three feet away from her, P's body laid in a pool of his blood. "What did you dooo?..."

On her knees, Roxy asked a rhetorical question before she buried her face into the palms of her own hand.

Boc! Boc!

"Shut up bitch!" Keem silenced the sound of Roxy's voice by placing two bullets through the skull of her head. He tucked his heated pistol and stepped over Roxy's stiff corpse. "Don't ask me no ma fuckin questions. Bitch," he mumbled to himself while heading towards the door. "That's yo' ma'fuckin problem now. If you would've jus answered the fucking question, yo' ass could—" Keem made his exit out of the front door. Turning Roxy's crib into a funeral home, he left her living room painted with rose red floors.

**

At the gated entrance of the APTs on the top of the hill in Mosby, BM held a meeting. One that would establish his control. Tonight, he would build the proper foundation to his structure. He had somehow finessed his way into two apartment hallways that were at the entrance of the APTs on both sides. This was one of his missions from the beginning. With that location, he could control who came into the apartments and watched who left out. Wisely though, he wanted to lay low until other parts of his plan was placed together. He understood that he was one of Mosby's least favorites, especially with his latest chain of actions. That, along with the facts of his reputation, he knew that if his presence was to be known, it would unquestionably alarm his rivals. So, he would lay dormant in the grass until it was time to strike.

"Y'all lil niggas been handling business outchea. I respect that. Roll up!" BM tossed an ounce of weed on the table.

"Damn! Thats that pressure," one of the little peons stated.

"Hell yeah nigga, Za." BM confirmed. "I call that shit Money Bag." The youngins laughed at the humor that was rarely in BM. There were six youngins seated at the table. A chair at the head of the table was empty. That was BM's seat. The other four occupants in the kitchen either sat or leaned against the countertop. "From now on, that's all y'all lil niggas smoking on. Is the best. Y'all wanna upgrade yo' drip?"

"Hell yeah," most of them answered with unity.

"Then y'all gon' do it with the best. Designer errthing," BM spoke with authority. The way he expressed his words made them believe him. "When it's time to pull up, y'all gon' do that shit in the latest whips. And if yo' hustle really right, y'all can pull up in something foreign."

It's amazing what an ounce of weed and a few dreams for sell could manipulate the minds of the immature. "We 'bout to take this bitch over. And it starts right here. Y'all know how it goes. Take over The Hill and the rest of the projects gone fall in line. Plus, the best part for us is that, we already running the Bottom. Ain't no niggas did it like we about to do this shit."

All the faces were focused. Deeply intrigued in the speech of their potential ends coming in. If it was dreams that BM was selling, they were all buying. BM picked the lowest of the low. True savages that had nothing to lose. Most of the pack was already satisfied with just the short distance that they've succeed in success. Now here BM was, promising more. Dangling raw steak in the face of the cubs. Leading them to only a place that he knew. He pulled a bookbag from out of one of the kitchen cabinets. Then, dumped the contents on the kitchen table in front of everyone. It was thirty thousand dollars, straight street money. It was drug money in its lowest form. There were barely any bill present over a twenty-dollar bill. With that being said to the young eyes, the amount of money looked larger than it really was.

"This thirty bands," BM announced, stating the number only enticed the young members more. Not once did they think of thirty thousand being split between the eleven of them. They all had in mind the money being only their own. Hell, one thousand dollars was enough for the low lives to think of themselves as being rich. So just imagine the images they held in their minds at the time about the thirty bands.

"Oh shit. Thirty gang!" A youngin shouted out in celebration with a thirty-shot clip resting in his lap. Let's just call him Shoota for an alias. Most of his other peers got a good laugh out if his sarcasm.

"Damn right," BM agreed as he dapped the youngin Shoota up for more motivation. "I grind this shit up from three bullshit ass bands with a lil help from the gang of course," he said blowing their heads up even more like an inflatable.

"You already know nigga," one of the best young hustlers on the team assured. For future reference, we'll call him Bank.

"From thirty hundred to thirty thousand in less than thirty days," BM continued after nodding at Bank. "And I still ain't satisfied. And y'all shouldn't be either." Neither of them had anything to say. "We 'bout to turn this thirty thousand into three hundred thousand." Their voices remained silent, but the looks on their faces said it all. Some faces expressed major disbelief. BM wrote them off automatically as weak links. He placed them in the category as pawns. A few faces were fascinated by the thought. BM would give them the positions of rooks and bishops. For the couple who watched with intensified interest, BM mentally laid the sword on both on each of both of their shoulders, dubbing them the knights.

"I see some of y'all lookin at me like I'm crazy." BM chuckled lightly. "Like y'all lil niggas ain't got no dreams or some. Like y'all ain't got shit to live for out this bitch!" His voice was growing more sinister by the second. "Luckily for y'all lil ma'fuckas I'ma give y'all a purpose. But if y'all prove to be useless, then I'ma give you some to die for."

"I'm down with whatever," a minor at the age of sixteen said. His name was Tru. "But how you expect us to trust these niggas?" Tru was actually E's cousin. He was only a small part of BM's grand scheme of things. The niggas he felt that were untrustworthy were the three Creighton youngins that were hovering by the countertops.

"Cuz I say so. They already proved themselves. You think I'll be stupid enough to have them round if I didn't? Matter of fact—" BM paused, holding his chin as he looked up at the ceiling. "Y'all ain't gotta trust 'em. Just trust me," he said that as if he was trustworthy himself. Because little did any of them knew, BM would not hesitate for one second to sacrifice any of his pieces to make sure he made it to the top. His plans were concrete. And his will was determined to execute those plans. It was just his intention that was so ill.

His first step was to outgrow Pike as his plug. He needed someone with heavier weight. And he knew just the person.

LESSON 1.22
All Money Is Legal Money

"You don't have to lie E'Vel." Crawford was showing off her freshly done nails. The colors were a mixture of olive green and a light sand tan. "If you don't like 'em, I can get 'em done ova. I just wanted to try some different. And plus, the colors match my uniform."

"You know I like different. But why you don't believe me when I say I like 'em?" E was leaning over the horseshoe where the CO's would station themselves.

"I do believe you. I just had to double check to make sure you wasn't lying."

"How many times have you caught me lying?"

"None," Crawford shyly said with a light blush.

"Aight then," E responded. "You don't ever have to waste your time double checking my honesty."

"I know that boo. I'm sorry."

Tiara Crawford was a native from Cleveland, Ohio. She was new to Virginia and here with a brand-new plan. This was the third different jail that she had worked at. The first time she had took drugs into a jail, it was through an introduction of an inmate that soon became her boyfriend. Due to a flamboyant lack of discipline, their run was cut short. Being that her superiors had no physical evidence, besides of word of mouth, she was let off the hook with just being fired. Sparing her of the criminal charges that could have been brought up against her.

From there, she traveled to Cincinnati or a fresh start. Being short on cash only turned up her determination to hustle harder. Wisely, she learned from her last situation to reframe from allowing her heart to get involved. Another lesson learned was to put some money up. That was mandatory and nonnegotiable. She succeeded at putting a few dollars up. It wasn't much though. And believe it or not, but her rule of removing her heart from the hustle backfired on her. The next nigga she had chosen was a cold, tender dick sucker. He made Tiara regret that she ever gave him a chance. He grew jealous when other inmates talked or even looked at her. He tried to control what she spent her portion of the money on, while barely cutting the pie evenly. The straw that broke the camel's back was when he got in a secluded area and attempted to take the pussy from her. She promised a lie that if he did, she would risk her own freedom to make sure he was tried and convicted of rape. It scared him off. And scared her away.

That's what landed her in the land of Virginia. She promised herself that this would be her last run. Therefore, she knew no other option but to make it count. And so far she had no complaints. Actually, it was going a little too good for comfort.

E was like a nigga she had never met before. Her heart was uncontrollably developing deepen emotions for him. So much so, that it scared her. In fact, it scared her so much that she even considered falling back from the whole operation. On the other hand, though, there just wasn't a logical reason to. Everything that she had asked for business wise had manifested with her meeting E. It's just that he also happened to be the man of her dreams. Characteristic wise, morals, and looks.

"I made a new Cashapp for you too," Crawford stated.

"I know," E replied with confidence. "What is it?"

"Boy, how you know that?" Crawford asked with a laugh. "And it's PUFF$. The S is a dollar sign. All caps."

169

"I know that because by now I know you about yo' business. And what the fuck is PUFF$?"

"It's abbreviation for Pay Up Front For Strips."

"Ooohhh. Shawty you clever as hell." Crawford blushed a little more. She loved when E called her shawty in addition to a comment. "I'ma set up a few more plays to the Cashapp we using now and then we gone scrap it."

Within the first couple weeks together, they had accumulated a little over eight thousand dollars. E wasn't too seriously pressed for cash, even though he started off broke. Therefore, he split the bread with Crawford on the receiving end of the seven thousand dollars. He collected the rest. E was tapping into his ultimate hustle. He hadn't even spent a dollar of his share of the money. Along with the grind he had going with Crawford, he also had his own. Selling commissary was one of the main ones. It allowed him to keep a load of food in his cell without having to go to the jail's store.

"Open the door right quick for me. I'ma go get these tray carts and push them up front." With the assistance of Crawford, E had upped his clout high enough in the jail to assign himself a job. He just needed a little wiggle room to maneuver through the jail. Or at least the fifth floor, to build his clientele. Crawford did as she was asked as she always did. She grew confident that E wouldn't mislead her at all. She was right too. E's first priority was to keep Crawford safe. He understood how valuable she was.

"Be back in a few," E assured as he pushed the lunch cart through the double doors. He went down the hallway and stopped at Unit 5-F that was right beside his. He pounded his fist on the closed door looking to get attention of the CO. The woman looked back with the facial expression asking 'What the hell you want' even though she already knew.

"Open the door!" E demanded. She did. He walked through the doors that were sliding open with the push of a

CRIME PAYS | SELF MADE TAY

button. As he entered the tier, he reached for the tray cart that was most likely filled with empty lunch trays.

"E!" Someone yelled on the tier as soon as he was spotted. "Thats a touchdown." The man confirmed.

"Already. Yall niggas better go for a two-point conversion," E replied back to the code.

"Aight that's a bet." E sticking strictly to the business, never out wore his welcome when it came to the inches he was giving. Walking behind the cart, he pushed it up towards the beginning of the hallway. There was another station for the sergeant ranked CO sat overseeing the tiers on the fifth floor. "Sup Rawlings?" He spoke out of respect for the female sergeant.

"How you doin' Foster? You staying out of trouble?"

"Yeah, I got to." E admitted.

"You better. You going to get the rest of the carts, right?" The question was rhetorical. It was mainly for the sake of conversation.

"You know I got cha."

"I know."

By the time E had finished bringing the final tray cart to the front of the hall, one of the two elevators were pulling up to the fifth floor. The door dinged and out popped Flex.

"Aye Lil E! What's up nigga?" Flex was full of energy. His eyes expressed a man on a mission. He felt no need to make an introduction because people that didn't even know him knew of him.

"Anderson!" Rawlings yelled at Flex. "What the fuck are you doing on this floor? Yo' ass is supposed to be downstairs."

"Naw I came to help put the tray carts on the elevator," Flex lied quickly in response.

"Boy yo' ass do not work in the kitchen. Get yo' ass back on that elevator and get downstairs."

171

"Aight. I got you. Hold on—" Flex placed sergeant Rawlings on hold and turned his attention back towards E. "A nigga tryna score a touchdown fool. What's the play."

E was stuck for a minute damn near dumbfounded. Of course, he knew of Flex. Although he was from the opposite side, he respected and looked up to Flex. Being in Flex's presence for the first time made E feel as if he had risen to another level. Yet, still, E did what he did best. He kept his cool.

"PUFF$, niggas all cap."

"PUFF$? Niggas all cap?" Flex mumbled to himself.

E noticed that Flex looked a little confused. "Smoke green fool," E said to throw the CO off, hoping not to confuse Flex any further.

It took Flex a few seconds to calculate it in his mind. But soon, he was able to put it all together.

"Ooohhh— PUFF$, niggas all cap." He finally figured it out. "Aye that's a fact though."

"No bullshit." E confirmed. "Big cap! All caps! But aye, go long and I'ma Hail Mary the ball."

"Aight bet. Say no more fool. Aye—" Flex pumped his arm muscle. "This purple heart. Thats me."

E thought for a quick second before he realized he was talking about emojis. "Already brah. I got you fool. I'ma send word when I view you."

"Already." Flex ended the business conversation with E before turning to flirt with the CO. "I love you Rawlings."

"Boy bye." She acted as if she didn't like it. Just like that, Flex was gone. "You goin' back in Foster?" She asked E who was already walking back to the unit.

"Yeah. Hit the door for me please."

"I got you. Thank you and stay out of trouble."

"You already know.

" Once E was back on the tier, Crawford had just finished making a round. They met each other at the horseshoe.

"And what took you so long?" She questioned him with a hint of jealousy.

"Naw, I had just made another play in the hallway. Nigga was from downstairs."

"Umm-hmm. Don't play."

"I ain't playing," he assured her, "About that bread."

"I'm talking 'bout me."

"I know what you talking about. The only way I'm tryna play with you is with my tongue playing ring around the rosy on that pussy." Crawford blushed again. But she didn't have much to say. She felt like child having their first crush. Like I said, her plan wasn't to fall in love. But she was falling head over heels. Like a waterfall diving into a sea of love.

***

Mac, Chop, and Blade sat parked in the car waiting underneath the bridge. Blade was behind the wheel, Chop in the passenger seat, with Mac in the backseat as always.

"There go that fool right there boss," Chop said to Mac as he watched the car pull up to the front end of the vehicle they occupied.

"You know what to do." Was all Mac said. Without another word, Chop hopped out the car and met their awaiting guest face to face. He knew the routine. Lifting his arms up, he stood still allowing Chop to pat him down in a search for weapons. Once clear, Chop allowed the man to travel ahead of him as he escorted him to the car that Mac awaited in. Chop opened the door to the backseat of the car. The man climbed in, taking a seat beside Mac.

"Macsby." The man greeted calling Mac by his last name.

"Detective," Mac responded with a nonchalant tone.

"You got what I came for?" The detective was a medium height about 5' 7". A white man with a low-cut brunette color hair.

"For you to be so smart, that was a dumb ass question. Package!" On demand Chop was handing Mac an envelope that contained one hundred one-hundred-dollar bills. Mac handed it over to the detective who reached for it. Mac suddenly snatched it back. "Slow down, now you know the deal."

"Well, it's the same spill. Calvez is still begging me to dig up shit on you. Other than suspicion, he doesn't have anything physically on you." The detective began to give the run down, keeping Mac a few steps ahead of the law. "But he has been on to something that just may fall back on you. You know, like a domino effect type shit. Thats if you give a shit."

"Okay. And what's that?" Mac was all ears.

"Your son." Mac released a sigh at the sound of his weakest link. "Yeah." The detective clearly understood. "Calvez has been keeping a close eye on him. He has reason to believe that your son BM was involved with the robbery of that corner store right around New Years. Also, Calvez suspects that your son was involved in the shooting of the E'Vel kid. But of course, we've already discussed that."

"Exactly," Mac said as a matter of fact. "So, out with the old. In with the new."

"Right." The detective moved on to the next. "It seems as if yo' son is following in his father's footsteps."

"Meaning?" Mac was unsure of the exact meaning to the detective's words.

"He's putting a crew together. Looks like he's taking a shot at the King of the Hill."

"What?" Mac was fully alert now.

"Yep. The kid is relentless. Willing and ready to knock off anybody that gets in his way. Word of mouth says that Calvez and his partner were right in the area when BM had assumingly murdered the young boy on Mosby Street. The kid was from Hillside went by the street name, Crow. He was only sixteen. His friend was wounded badly as well. Lil One,

CRIME PAYS | SELF MADE TAY

they call him. Calvez has been trying to get both E and Lil One to confess that BM was their attempted murderer. But neither are saying a thing. Aside from that, BM has been on a hustling marathon. Nothing too big. But definitely bigger than his usual. Just something to keep a watch on."

"Thank you for the report Detective. Is that all?"

"For now, yes. If anything comes up, I'll set a meeting. Til then, I'll continue to mislead Calvez. But you might wanna get a leash on yo' kid," the detective suggested.

Mac hated the fact that the detective was right on the advice that he gave him. But he couldn't be arrogant and turn a blind eye to the situation. To Mac, BM wasn't quite a problem yet. But he was like a hurricane developing in the ocean, soon to make its way to the land.

A ring erupted from someone's phone. It was the detective's. "Gibson speaking," he answered. "Really? Okay. I'm on my way." Detective Gibson hung the phone up and placed it back into his pockets. "Aight Macsby, gotta go. Some of us actually does honest work out here."

"Yeah, and yo' honest work is the same thing that got you outchea side hustling for dirty money. But it's cool though, I ain't gone knock you and I definitely can't judge you. See you later." Mac had a sound understanding about life. He didn't believe in all that good and bad shit. To him it was all the same really. There wasn't one without the other.

Detective Gibson exited the car and hastily got to his. He hopped behind the wheel of the car peeling the tires kicking up dust clouds over the dirt pavement. Speaking of the revenging devil himself, Gibson was on his way to Calvez. Good thing he wasn't far away. He was pulling up to the scene in no time at all.

Forensics, paramedics, and the coroner was already there alongside Detective Calvez and Winchester. The dock was closed off with caution tape.

"What's the spill?" Gibson asked as he climbed out of the car putting on his best work impression.

"That was fast," Calvez responded. He waited for a few seconds waiting for Gibson to duck underneath the tape. As he did, he heard a bump. Something was banging beneath the dock. Each time the water splashed from the James River; it caused the object to bang into the dock again. "Well." Calvez continued. "Got a call from a fisherman, said something was fishy under the dock." Calvez paused taking a look at the two detectives, waiting to see if he would catch on to his joke. They just looked on with serious stares. "No sense of humors? Anyway, we got a body under there floating. You're just in time too. The forensic team is pulling it out now."

The three stood by as the large net pulled the body from under the dock and out of the water. The team of men guided the body over the dock and laid it on top off it.

"Well, well, well—" Calvez repeated. "She looks familiar, doesn't she partner?"

"Sure does." Winchester confirmed. "It's the—" He started to say.

"Woman from the Macsby stakeout." Calvez and Winchester finished the sentence together.

"You think so?" Winchester questioned examining the corpse with his eyes only, head tilted slightly to the side.

"Hard to tell right now." Calvez responded truthfully.

"Doesn't really seem like there's any bodily harm done to the body," Gibson stated as if he was routing for there to be none.

"We'll let the autopsy go through. Let them be the judge of that. Then, we'll go from there. That way we'll have the factual evidence," Calvez advised as he begun to head off the dock. "Until then, I'm going to attempt to give our Lil One a scare. See if I can get him to tell us what happened here. Or at least give us a bit of a hint. Let's go partner." The couple of team detectives walked off leaving Gibson on the dock the along to ponder.

LESSON 1.23
The Game Goes On

"I swear sir. I have not the first idea of who would wanna do this to her. I loved her with all my heart, sir." Derek was talking to a police officer, who was checking for a report for the second time since Kimberly's murder. "Don't you think that if I had any idea, I would have clarified that by now?" Truthfully, Derek was extremely remorseful. His regrets ate away at his conscious. But he was forced to keep his truths buried beneath his illusions. What else was he supposed to do? Become an Honest Abe and incriminate himself? What was done was done. There was no undoing it now.

What motivated him to keep the cat in the bag was convincing himself that Kimberly got exactly what she deserved. Derek treated her as best as he could. Kimberly treated him like shit, carelessly flushing his feelings down the toilet. Thinking back on all the pain and betrayal was the only thing that snapped him of his emotions of love.

There was a sense of fear that shivered the bones of Derek's body. For the life of him, he couldn't figure out what possessed him to allow and even aid the assistance of the love of his life murder. Was hate that powerful that one would cut branches off it's own family's tree? To keep his sanity, Derek had to constantly feed his subconscious the cold thoughts of that same hatred. He thought that it was getting by. Little did he know those same cold thoughts were leaking down towards his heart.

"I understand, sir," the officer replied. He held a pen and a pad in his hands, taking notes of basically nothing. "Just doing my job. And again, I'm sorry for your loss. Have a good day." The officer turned and headed down the few steps exiting the porch. Derek walked back in his apartment, closed the door, and flopped down on the couch.

For quite some time, Derek sat stationed on the couch staring. Trying to see through all the static in his brain, he had no sense of control in his life. Everything was out of order for him. His mind flashed to Shawndra. He questioned if she was having the same feelings about Tank. Maybe that's what he needed. Someone who would understand. Who was better to understand him at a moment like this other than her. He snatched up the keys and headed for the door.

In seven minutes of time, he was pulling up to Shawndra's street. Contemplating on rather he should go through with his decision or not, Derek remained in the car. His feet moved him to her front door. Once there, he knocked on it. After waiting longer than the usual visitor, Derek wanted to leave from in front of the door, he just didn't have the energy to do so. His mental and emotional drainage were both wearing on his physical.

Inside the apartment, right beside the door, Shawndra sat on the couch hugging on a pillow. She was going through a mental breakdown herself. She thought that letting the tears of her soul flow would rid her emotions of all the pain. But even a pillow full of tears couldn't wipe the pain away.

She ignored the knock on the door, hoping that whoever that it was would go away. She had completely no energy to give. After the extra-long pause, she just assumed that the unwanted guest had just went away. To her own surprise, she found out that she was wrong when the knock eventually repeated itself. That struck Shawndra's curiosity. She wondered who was so patient. So persistent. So desperate. Climbing up slightly off the couch, Shawndra snuck a look out of the window.

Once she noticed it was Derek, a stream of electricity shot through her body. She was literally shocked. She jolted off the couch and brushed her fuzzy hair down with her hands. Automatically deciding to allow Derek in, she reached for the door handle. Right before grasping it, she pulled back. "What is you doin' Shawn?" She whispered the question to herself. Before she could even put up a self debate, her hand was twisting the handle and yanking the door open.

"Hey." Shawndra's voice was nervous and girly like.

Derek didn't even notice that he was doing it, but he walked right into the apartment. "Can I come in?" He asked after already being in.

"Umm… sure. I guess," Shawndra stated as if she had an option to say no. "Come right on in." She closed and locked the door before turning to face Derek. When she did, she saw that he was standing in front of the fish tank staring into the clear waters. "You okay?" She knew the question was a tricky one to answer. But was really referring to his weird actions and not his recent feelings.

Derek sniffed up the snot that was sliding through his nose. "I don't know what to do." From the sound of his voice, Shawndra could tell that he was welling up in tears. He sounded pathetic. "Why did you do it?" He asked before turning around to face her. His face was soaked with emotions. "Why did you go through with it?"

Shawndra was starting to realize that she may have made a mistake that could possibly backfire on her. Not with the murders. But with allowing Derek inside her home. What the fuck was she thinking? "I had too," she stated. Honestly though, she wasn't the one behind the gun that murdered Kimberly. "If I wouldn't have went through with the plan, Tank's crazy ass would've killed all of us."

She most likely was right. Derek would just have to get over it. Besides, he may have not have made the bed, but he definitely provided the blanket and sheets. His soul was just as stained as hers.

179

"Come here." Shawndra stepped closer to Derek slowly. He remained standing still. She wrapped her arms around his neck and softly pulled him closer. With one hand, she cradled the back of his head and buried his face in the nape of her neck. "We're gonna have to get through this together."

For a timely moment, Derek was tense, which caused him to remain stiff. But soon the softness of her body placed his body slowly at ease. Her warmth raised up the temperature of his cold thoughts. The sweet fragrance of her skin awoke him to the vitals of life. She was right. There was no way that he would be able to get through this alone. Maybe they could share each other's pain until the healing came. Derek wrapped his arms around Shawndra and embraced her fully. "Thank you," he said so low that it was barely audible.

Shawndra left the words of gratitude unresponsive. She lowered her hands and removed Derek's hands from around her lower back. "Take a seat," she offered while guiding him towards the couch. He did. "Give me a minute. I'll be right back." Derek remained silent. Shawndra headed up the flight of stairs. Shortly, she returned with a gym bag. She took a seat beside Derek on the couch, leaving enough space to sit the bag in between them. "I think it's about fifty-thousand dollars in this bag. I don't know much about yo' lifestyle, but there's also drugs in here and I have absolutely no need for them. It was his."

Confused, Derek was speechless. Could the money take the pain away? Was this all his Kimberly's life was worth? Was she really that worthless? "We can split it," Derek suggested. Only though because he didn't want to take advantage of her.

"No." Shawndra denied his offer. "I've already taken out what I needed. This yours. You can use it to help with yo' son. It's the least I could do. So, please accept it."

Derek dropped his head down and looked towards the floor. That baby is not mine," Derek confessed. "Kimberly had that baby while we were together. True enough, I accepted the baby but it's not biologically mine. I don't know who that baby's father is. Hell, it could have been Tank's for all I know." The breaking news touched Shawndra's heart. She looked at Derek in even a higher moral character than even before. Derek was grateful for Shawndra's unselfish thoughtfulness. She could have been greedy and not thought about him at all. He looked from the bag of money and up into Shawndra's eyes. The sincerity was evident. She made eye contact with him and matched his stare. The energy between the two was vibrating rapidly. So much so, that it was almost as if they could hear each other's thoughts.

Without saying a word, they launched at each other passionately. Their lips locked and their tongues met. Shawndra released a moan while rubbing her hand along Derek's masculine jaw line. There was nothing she needed more than to release her bottled-up emotions. She felt that there was no one better to be so transparent with than the one who felt her the most. They were all over each other like long-time lovers. It wasn't long before Shawndra pulled off Derek's jacket and lifted up his shirt. For a lustrous second, she admired his upper muscles desiring to be held in his strength. She rubbed her hands down his chest to his six pack. Her body shivered from the sexual anticipation.

Taking charge, Derek threw the bag on the floor and laid Shawndra down on the couch. He wanted to taste her. He kissed her on her full succulent lips and made his way down to her neck, placing kisses every inch of the way. Softly and slowly, he licked her on the neck. The taste of her skin satisfied his sensation. Lightly, he sucked on it. Shawndra moaned seductively while grasping Derek in her arms. Rubbing her hands all over his back, he moved down to her breasts. Kissing her erected nipples through her chiffon silk pajama top, he rubbed and massaged them through the fabric. The feeling moving against her skin aroused her more.

CRIME PAYS | SELF MADE TAY

Continuing to make his way down, Derek lifted her shirt to the top of her stomach. He placed more kisses on her bare skin, making his way below her belly button. He could smell his nose getting closer to the pussy. It smelled like a garden of roses that was sprayed over with Bath and Body Works products. He pulled down her pajama's shorts. And now, I guess you could say that the cat was out of the bag. As the shorts made it to her ankles, Shawndra withdrew her bare feet from the pajamas. She spread her legs wide and begged Derek to dive in. He did. Headfirst.

It was as if he'd bitten into a peachy cream filled piece of chocolate. Like one of the one you get out of those heart shaped Valentines Day boxes. True indeed, Valentines Day was drawing near, but it felt as if cupid was already here. Lust was subconsciously transforming into love.

Derek ate up her pussy like it was plate of spaghetti and he had no fork. The taste was magnificent. Her juices were fluid. It soaked his facial hairs. Shawndra gripped his head messing up his wave's as the waves of emotions flooded through her. His tongue magnified her electricity. Every lick of the tongue touched her soul. Damn near had her speaking in tongues.

"Fuck me, please!" Shawndra demanded the dick. She couldn't take it any longer. The head was good but she urged for the feeling of being filled. She pulled Derek up by his ears and he complied. With both of their late mates cheating on them, along with the fact that they knew about the affairs, it's honestly been a while since either of them had any sexual relations.

Derek planked himself over Shawndra. She immediately reached for his hardened dick and massaged it with her soft hands. To Derek, it felt amazing. Shawndra then guided his dick head to the opening of her pussy. Her lips were wet, warm, soft, and slippery. The feelings made his knees weak just from the contact. Slowly, yet firmly Derek pushed his dick a little further into her body. She cringed with a sigh at the bittersweet feeling. Looking into Shawndra's eyes, Derek eased his way out and then when it was least expected, shifted his direction and went forward again. Shawndra's eyes widened from surprise. She wrapped her arms around Derek's body and pulled him in closer. The speed of Derek's strokes took pace. Their bodies clashed against each other causing slapping sounds to echo throughout the apartment. She dug her natural nails into his back. Derek continued to poke her box. His eyes roamed from her nipples and from her flattened stomach. He just couldn't keep his eyes off her. The way her titties bounced as he now slammed his dick inside of her.

"Yes. Fuck me!" The sweet sound of her voice matched her fragrance. The passion. The connection. The energy. It all just…

"Uhhggg—" Derek was exploding semen into Shawndra's pussy. The ejaculation weakened his body. But the pursuit of passion lead him to an attempt to keep pumping. He didn't want to exit the moment or passion they shared.

Shawndra was turned on even more by Derek's second effort. She pulled him in as close as she could and wrapped her legs around his waist. She thrust her pelvis area and whined her hips in circular rotating motions. By this time, Derek had collapsed on top of her. For now, he just couldn't take anymore, but he wasn't leaving until he mustered up enough energy to go another round. He was pleased but wouldn't feel complete until he pleased her. For now, he just laid his head on her breast. The sex was good to Shawndra, but what she wanted more than anything at that moment was to be wrapped up in his arms. To be loved and protected. Safe and sound. She brushed his waves over with her hands, closed her eyes and cherished the moment.

To Be Continued…

Lock Down Publications and Ca$h Presents
Assisted Publishing Packages

BASIC PACKAGE	UPGRADED PACKAGE
$499	$800
Editing	Typing
Cover Design	Editing
Formatting	Cover Design
	Formatting
ADVANCE PACKAGE	**LDP SUPREME PACKAGE**
$1,200	$1,500
Typing	Typing
Editing	Editing
Cover Design	Cover Design
Formatting	Formatting
Copyright registration	Copyright registration
Proofreading	Proofreading
Upload book to Amazon	Set up Amazon account
	Upload book to Amazon
	Advertise on LDP, Amazon and Facebook Page

***Other services available upon request.
Additional charges may apply

Lock Down Publications
P.O. Box 944
Stockbridge, GA 30281-9998
Phone: 470 303-9761

Submission Guideline

Submit the first three chapters of your completed manuscript to ldpsubmissions@gmail.com. In the subject line add **Your Book's Title**. The manuscript must be in a Word Doc file and sent as an attachment. Document should be in Times New Roman, double spaced, and in size 12 font. Also, provide your synopsis and full contact information. If sending multiple submissions, they must each be in a separate email.

Have a story but no way to send it electronically? You can still submit to LDP/Ca$h Presents. Send in the first three chapters, written or typed, of your completed manuscript to:

LDP: Submissions Dept
P.O. Box 944
Stockbridge, GA 30281-9998

DO NOT send original manuscript. Must be a duplicate. Provide your synopsis and a cover letter containing your full contact information.

Thanks for considering LDP and Ca$h Presents.

NEW RELEASES

BLOODLINE OF A SAVAGE **BY PRINCE A. TAUHID**

THE MURDER QUEENS 4 **BY MICHAEL GALLON**

THE BUTTERFLY MAFIA **BY FUMIYA PAYNE**

KING KILLA 2 **BY VINCENT "VITTO" HOLLOWAY**

BABY, I'M WINTERTIME COLD 3 **BY MEESHA**

THESE VICIOUS STREETS **BY PRINCE A. TAUHID**

TIL DEATH 2 **BY ARYANNA**

CITY OF SMOKE 2 **BY MOLOTTI**

STEPPERS **BY KING RIO**

THE LANE **BY KEN-KEN SPENCE**

MONEY GAME 2 **BY SMOOVE DOLLA**

THE BLACK DIAMOND CARTEL **BY SAYNOMORE**

CRIME BOSS 2 **BY PLAYA RAY**

THUG OF SPADES **BY COREY ROBINSON**

LOVE IN THE TRENCHES 2 **BY COREY ROBINSON**

TIL DEATH 3 **BY ARYANNA**

THE BIRTH OF A GANGSTER 4 **BY DELMONT PLAYER**

PRODUCT OF THE STREETS **BY DEMOND "MONEY" ANDERSON**

Coming Soon from Lock Down Publications/Ca$h Presents

BLOOD OF A BOSS VI
SHADOWS OF THE GAME II
TRAP BASTARD II
By **Askari**

LOYAL TO THE GAME IV
By **T.J. & Jelissa**

TRUE SAVAGE VIII
MIDNIGHT CARTEL IV
DOPE BOY MAGIC IV
CITY OF KINGZ III
NIGHTMARE ON SILENT AVE II
THE PLUG OF LIL MEXICO II
CLASSIC CITY II
By **Chris Green**

BLAST FOR ME III
A SAVAGE DOPEBOY III
CUTTHROAT MAFIA III
DUFFLE BAG CARTEL VII
HEARTLESS GOON VI
By **Ghost**

A HUSTLER'S DECEIT III
KILL ZONE II
BAE BELONGS TO ME III
TIL DEATH II
By **Aryanna**

KING OF THE TRAP III
By **T.J. Edwards**

GORILLAZ IN THE BAY V
3X KRAZY III
STRAIGHT BEAST MODE III
By **De'Kari**

KINGPIN KILLAZ IV
STREET KINGS III
PAID IN BLOOD III
CARTEL KILLAZ IV
DOPE GODS III
By **Hood Rich**

SINS OF A HUSTLA II
By **ASAD**

YAYO V
BRED IN THE GAME 2
By **S. Allen**

THE STREETS WILL TALK II
By **Yolanda Moore**

SON OF A DOPE FIEND III
HEAVEN GOT A GHETTO III
SKI MASK MONEY III
By **Renta**

LOYALTY AIN'T PROMISED III
By **Keith Williams**

I'M NOTHING WITHOUT HIS LOVE II
SINS OF A THUG II
TO THE THUG I LOVED BEFORE II
IN A HUSTLER I TRUST II
By **Monet Dragun**

QUIET MONEY IV
EXTENDED CLIP III
THUG LIFE IV
By **Trai'Quan**

THE STREETS MADE ME IV
By **Larry D. Wright**

IF YOU CROSS ME ONCE III
ANGEL V
By **Anthony Fields**

THE STREETS WILL NEVER CLOSE IV
By **K'ajji**

HARD AND RUTHLESS III
KILLA KOUNTY IV
By **Khufu**

MONEY GAME III
By **Smoove Dolla**

MURDA WAS THE CASE III
Elijah R. Freeman

AN UNFORESEEN LOVE IV
BABY, I'M WINTERTIME COLD III
By **Meesha**

QUEEN OF THE ZOO III
By **Black Migo**

CONFESSIONS OF A JACKBOY III
By **Nicholas Lock**

JACK BOYS VS DOPE BOYS IV
A GANGSTA'S QUR'AN V
COKE GIRLZ II
COKE BOYS II
LIFE OF A SAVAGE V
CHI'RAQ GANGSTAS V
SOSA GANG III
BRONX SAVAGES II
BODYMORE KINGPINS II
By **Romell Tukes**

KING KILLA II
By **Vincent "Vitto" Holloway**

BETRAYAL OF A THUG III
By **Fre$h**

THE MURDER QUEENS III
By **Michael Gallon**

THE BIRTH OF A GANGSTER III
By **Delmont Player**

TREAL LOVE II
By **Le'Monica Jackson**

FOR THE LOVE OF BLOOD III
By **Jamel Mitchell**

RAN OFF ON DA PLUG II
By **Paper Boi Rari**

HOOD CONSIGLIERE III
By **Keese**

PRETTY GIRLS DO NASTY THINGS II
By **Nicole Goosby**

PROTÉGÉ OF A LEGEND III
LOVE IN THE TRENCHES II
By **Corey Robinson**

IT'S JUST ME AND YOU II
By **Ah'Million**

FOREVER GANGSTA III
By **Adrian Dulan**

GORILLAZ IN THE TRENCHES II
By **SayNoMore**

THE COCAINE PRINCESS VIII
By **King Rio**

CRIME BOSS II
By **Playa Ray**

LOYALTY IS EVERYTHING III
By **Molotti**

HERE TODAY GONE TOMORROW II
By **Fly Rock**

REAL G'S MOVE IN SILENCE II
By **Von Diesel**

GRIMEY WAYS IV
By **Ray Vinci**

Available Now

RESTRAINING ORDER I & II
By **CA$H & Coffee**

LOVE KNOWS NO BOUNDARIES I II & III
By **Coffee**

RAISED AS A GOON I, II, III & IV
BRED BY THE SLUMS I, II, III
BLAST FOR ME I & II
ROTTEN TO THE CORE I II III
A BRONX TALE I, II, III
DUFFLE BAG CARTEL I II III IV V VI
HEARTLESS GOON I II III IV V
A SAVAGE DOPEBOY I II
DRUG LORDS I II III
CUTTHROAT MAFIA I II
KING OF THE TRENCHES
By **Ghost**

LAY IT DOWN I & II
LAST OF A DYING BREED I II
BLOOD STAINS OF A SHOTTA I & II III
By **Jamaica**

LOYAL TO THE GAME I II III
LIFE OF SIN I, II III
By **TJ & Jelissa**

IF LOVING HIM IS WRONG…I & II
LOVE ME EVEN WHEN IT HURTS I II III
By **Jelissa**

CRIME PAYS | SELF MADE TAY

BLOODY COMMAS I & II
SKI MASK CARTEL I, II & III
KING OF NEW YORK I II, III IV V
RISE TO POWER I II III
COKE KINGS I II III IV V
BORN HEARTLESS I II III IV
KING OF THE TRAP I II
By **T.J. Edwards**

WHEN THE STREETS CLAP BACK I & II III
THE HEART OF A SAVAGE I II III IV
MONEY MAFIA I II
LOYAL TO THE SOIL I II III
By **Jibril Williams**

A DISTINGUISHED THUG STOLE MY HEART I II &
III
LOVE SHOULDN'T HURT I II III IV
RENEGADE BOYS I II III IV
PAID IN KARMA I II III
SAVAGE STORMS I II III
AN UNFORESEEN LOVE I II III
BABY, I'M WINTERTIME COLD I II
By **Meesha**

A GANGSTER'S CODE I &, II III
A GANGSTER'S SYN I II III
THE SAVAGE LIFE I II III
CHAINED TO THE STREETS I II III
BLOOD ON THE MONEY I II III
A GANGSTA'S PAIN I II III
By **J-Blunt**

PUSH IT TO THE LIMIT
By **Bre' Hayes**

BLOOD OF A BOSS I, II, III, IV, V
SHADOWS OF THE GAME
TRAP BASTARD
By **Askari**

THE STREETS BLEED MURDER I, II & III
THE HEART OF A GANGSTA I II& III
By **Jerry Jackson**

CUM FOR ME I II III IV V VI VII VIII
An **LDP Erotica Collaboration**

BRIDE OF A HUSTLA I II & II
THE FETTI GIRLS I, II& III
CORRUPTED BY A GANGSTA I, II III, IV
BLINDED BY HIS LOVE
THE PRICE YOU PAY FOR LOVE I, II ,III
DOPE GIRL MAGIC I II III
By **Destiny Skai**

WHEN A GOOD GIRL GOES BAD
By **Adrienne**

A GANGSTER'S REVENGE I II III & IV
THE BOSS MAN'S DAUGHTERS I II III IV V
A SAVAGE LOVE I & II
BAE BELONGS TO ME I II
A HUSTLER'S DECEIT I, II, III
WHAT BAD BITCHES DO I, II, III
SOUL OF A MONSTER I II III
KILL ZONE
A DOPE BOY'S QUEEN I II III
TIL DEATH
By **Aryanna**

THE COST OF LOYALTY I II III
By Kweli

A KINGPIN'S AMBITION
A KINGPIN'S AMBITION **II**
I MURDER FOR THE DOUGH
By **Ambitious**

TRUE SAVAGE I II III IV V VI VII
DOPE BOY MAGIC I, II, III
MIDNIGHT CARTEL I II III
CITY OF KINGZ I II
NIGHTMARE ON SILENT AVE
THE PLUG OF LIL MEXICO II
CLASSIC CITY
By **Chris Green**

A DOPEBOY'S PRAYER
By **Eddie "Wolf" Lee**

THE KING CARTEL I, II & III
By **Frank Gresham**

THESE NIGGAS AIN'T LOYAL I, II & III
By **Nikki Tee**

GANGSTA SHYT I II &III
By **CATO**

THE ULTIMATE BETRAYAL
By **Phoenix**

BOSS'N UP I, II & III
By **Royal Nicole**

CRIME PAYS | SELF MADE TAY

I LOVE YOU TO DEATH
By **Destiny J**

I RIDE FOR MY HITTA
I STILL RIDE FOR MY HITTA
By **Misty Holt**

LOVE & CHASIN' PAPER
By **Qay Crockett**

TO DIE IN VAIN
SINS OF A HUSTLA
By **ASAD**

BROOKLYN HUSTLAZ
By **Boogsy Morina**

BROOKLYN ON LOCK I & II
By **Sonovia**

GANGSTA CITY
By **Teddy Duke**

A DRUG KING AND HIS DIAMOND I & II III
A DOPEMAN'S RICHES
HER MAN, MINE'S TOO I, II
CASH MONEY HO'S
THE WIFEY I USED TO BE I II
PRETTY GIRLS DO NASTY THINGS
By Nicole Goosby

LIPSTICK KILLAH I, II, III
CRIME OF PASSION I II & III
FRIEND OR FOE I II III
By **Mimi**

TRAPHOUSE KING I II & III
KINGPIN KILLAZ I II III
STREET KINGS I II
PAID IN BLOOD I II
CARTEL KILLAZ I II III
DOPE GODS I II
By **Hood Rich**

STEADY MOBBN' I, II, III
THE STREETS STAINED MY SOUL I II III
By **Marcellus Allen**

WHO SHOT YA I, II, III
SON OF A DOPE FIEND I II
HEAVEN GOT A GHETTO I II
SKI MASK MONEY I II
By **Renta**

GORILLAZ IN THE BAY I II III IV
TEARS OF A GANGSTA I II
3X KRAZY I II
STRAIGHT BEAST MODE I II
By **DE'KARI**

TRIGGADALE I II III
MURDA WAS THE CASE I II
By **Elijah R. Freeman**

THE STREETS ARE CALLING
By **Duquie Wilson**

SLAUGHTER GANG I II III
RUTHLESS HEART I II III
By **Willie Slaughter**

CRIME PAYS | SELF MADE TAY

GOD BLESS THE TRAPPERS I, II, III
THESE SCANDALOUS STREETS I, II, III
FEAR MY GANGSTA I, II, III IV, V
THESE STREETS DON'T LOVE NOBODY I, II
BURY ME A G I, II, III, IV, V
A GANGSTA'S EMPIRE I, II, III, IV
THE DOPEMAN'S BODYGAURD I II
THE REALEST KILLAZ I II III
THE LAST OF THE OGS I II III
By **Tranay Adams**

MARRIED TO A BOSS I II III
By **Destiny Skai & Chris Green**

KINGZ OF THE GAME I II III IV V VI VII
CRIME BOSS
By **Playa Ray**

FUK SHYT
By **Blakk Diamond**

DON'T F#CK WITH MY HEART I II
By **Linnea**

ADDICTED TO THE DRAMA I II III
IN THE ARM OF HIS BOSS II
By **Jamila**

YAYO I II III IV
A SHOOTER'S AMBITION I II
BRED IN THE GAME
By **S. Allen**

LOYALTY AIN'T PROMISED I II
By **Keith Williams**

TRAP GOD I II III
RICH $AVAGE I II III
MONEY IN THE GRAVE I II III
By **Martell Troublesome Bolden**

FOREVER GANGSTA I II
GLOCKS ON SATIN SHEETS I II
By **Adrian Dulan**

TOE TAGZ I II III IV
LEVELS TO THIS SHYT I II
IT'S JUST ME AND YOU
By **Ah'Million**

KINGPIN DREAMS I II III
RAN OFF ON DA PLUG
By **Paper Boi Rari**

CONFESSIONS OF A GANGSTA I II III IV
CONFESSIONS OF A JACKBOY I II
By **Nicholas Lock**

I'M NOTHING WITHOUT HIS LOVE
SINS OF A THUG
TO THE THUG I LOVED BEFORE
A GANGSTA SAVED XMAS
IN A HUSTLER I TRUST
By **Monet Dragun**

QUIET MONEY I II III
THUG LIFE I II III
EXTENDED CLIP I II
A GANGSTA'S PARADISE
By **Trai'Quan**

CRIME PAYS | SELF MADE TAY

CAUGHT UP IN THE LIFE I II III
THE STREETS NEVER LET GO I II III
By **Robert Baptiste**

NEW TO THE GAME I II III
MONEY, MURDER & MEMORIES I II III
By **Malik D. Rice**

CREAM I II III
THE STREETS WILL TALK
By **Yolanda Moore**

LIFE OF A SAVAGE I II III IV
A GANGSTA'S QUR'AN I II III IV
MURDA SEASON I II III
GANGLAND CARTEL I II III
CHI'RAQ GANGSTAS I II III IV
KILLERS ON ELM STREET I II III
JACK BOYZ N DA BRONX I II III
A DOPEBOY'S DREAM I II III
JACK BOYS VS DOPE BOYS I II III
COKE GIRLZ
COKE BOYS
SOSA GANG I II
BRONX SAVAGES
BODYMORE KINGPINS
By **Romell Tukes**

THE STREETS MADE ME I II III
By **Larry D. Wright**

CONCRETE KILLA I II III
VICIOUS LOYALTY I II III
By **Kingpen**

THE ULTIMATE SACRIFICE I, II, III, IV, V, VI
KHADIFI
IF YOU CROSS ME ONCE I II
ANGEL I II III IV
IN THE BLINK OF AN EYE
By **Anthony Fields**

THE LIFE OF A HOOD STAR
By **Ca$h & Rashia Wilson**

THE STREETS WILL NEVER CLOSE I II III
By **K'ajji**

NIGHTMARES OF A HUSTLA I II III
By **King Dream**

HARD AND RUTHLESS I II
MOB TOWN 251
THE BILLIONAIRE BENTLEYS I II III
REAL G'S MOVE IN SILENCE
By **Von Diesel**

GHOST MOB
By **Stilloan Robinson**

MOB TIES I II III IV V VI
SOUL OF A HUSTLER, HEART OF A KILLER I II
GORILLAZ IN THE TRENCHES
By **SayNoMore**

BODYMORE MURDERLAND I II III
THE BIRTH OF A GANGSTER I II
By **Delmont Player**

CRIME PAYS | SELF MADE TAY

FOR THE LOVE OF A BOSS
By **C. D. Blue**

KILLA KOUNTY I II III IV
By Khufu

MOBBED UP I II III IV
THE BRICK MAN I II III IV V
THE COCAINE PRINCESS I II III IV V VI VII
By **King Rio**

MONEY GAME I II
By **Smoove Dolla**

A GANGSTA'S KARMA I II III
By **FLAME**

KING OF THE TRENCHES I II III
By **GHOST & TRANAY ADAMS**

QUEEN OF THE ZOO I II
By **Black Migo**

GRIMEY WAYS I II III
By **Ray Vinci**

XMAS WITH AN ATL SHOOTER
By **Ca$h & Destiny Skai**

KING KILLA
By **Vincent "Vitto" Holloway**

BETRAYAL OF A THUG I II
By **Fre$h**

CRIME PAYS | SELF MADE TAY

THE MURDER QUEENS I II
By **Michael Gallon**

TREAL LOVE
By **Le'Monica Jackson**

FOR THE LOVE OF BLOOD I II
By **Jamel Mitchell**

HOOD CONSIGLIERE I II
By **Keese**

PROTÉGÉ OF A LEGEND I II
LOVE IN THE TRENCHES
By **Corey Robinson**

BORN IN THE GRAVE I II III
By **Self Made Tay**

MOAN IN MY MOUTH
By **XTASY**

TORN BETWEEN A GANGSTER AND A
GENTLEMAN
By **J-BLUNT & Miss Kim**

LOYALTY IS EVERYTHING I II
By **Molotti**

HERE TODAY GONE TOMORROW
By **Fly Rock**

PILLOW PRINCESS
By **S. Hawkins**

CRIME PAYS | SELF MADE TAY

BOOKS BY LDP'S CEO, CA$H

TRUST IN NO MAN
TRUST IN NO MAN 2
TRUST IN NO MAN 3
BONDED BY BLOOD
SHORTY GOT A THUG
THUGS CRY
THUGS CRY 2
THUGS CRY 3
TRUST NO BITCH
TRUST NO BITCH 2
TRUST NO BITCH 3
TIL MY CASKET DROPS
RESTRAINING ORDER
RESTRAINING ORDER 2
IN LOVE WITH A CONVICT
LIFE OF A HOOD STAR
XMAS WITH AN ATL SHOOTER